# HATTIE ON HER WAY

# HATTIE ON HER WAY

## CLARA GILLOW CLARK

CANDLEWICK PRESS
CAMBRIDGE, MASSACHUSETTS

Copyright © 2005 by Clara Gillow Clark

First edition 2005

Library of Congress Cataloging-in-Publication Data

Clark, Clara Gillow.
Hattie on her way / Clara Gillow Clark. —1st ed.
p. cm.
Sequel to Hill Hawk Hattie.
Summary: In the late 1800s, eleven-year-old Hattie, still grieving over the death of
her mother and lonely for her absent father, moves in with her grandmother in the
city of Kingston, New York, to be educated and learn about polite society, and,
while there, discovers the fate of her missing grandfather.
ISBN 0-7636-2286-9
[1. Grandmothers—Fiction. 2. City and town life—Fiction.
3. Mental illness—Fiction. 4. Secrets—Fiction. 5. Conduct of life—Fiction.
6. Kingston (N.Y.)—History—1865–1898—Fiction.] I. Title.
PZ7.C5414Hat 2005
[fic]—dc22        2004051942

2 4 6 8 10 9 7 5 3 1

Printed in the United States of America

This book was typeset in Stempel Schneidler.

Candlewick Press
2067 Massachusetts Avenue
Cambridge, Massachusetts 02140

visit us at www.candlewick.com

*To Jamie Michalak*
*for being my corrective lenses and treasured friend*

*Heartfelt thanks to Mary Lee Donovan and*
*Andrea Tompa for being my eleventh-hour angels*

# APRIL 1883

# CHAPTER ONE

Pa said hawks don't crash into mountains or trees. He said they fly alert, watchful. But suppose a hawk got itself blown off course, ended up somewhere strange, somewhere it didn't rightly belong? Could it find its way home, fly back to its nest in the hills again? I'm wondering about that, 'cause I got blown off course—me, Hattie Belle Basket. When I wasn't suspecting a thing, Pa plunked me down in Kingston on the Hudson at Grandmother's fancy gingerbread house with brick walks and flower gardens and trellises. "You're my girl,

Hattie Belle, stronger than a hawk flying in a gale wind," Pa said. Then he left.

When he was nearly lost from sight, I whistled like a hawk to him, and he whistled back to signal that our real home was together. After that, I bit my lip real hard to keep a river of tears from flowing.

I decided to make the best of things here, because I knew that living with Grandmother was not forever. Things didn't seem too promising, though, after the way Grandmother sat stiff and straight as a bristle in her fancy rose-backed chair, her voice chilly as a killing frost, talking all pinch-nosed and proper to Pa. "Amos," she said, and stopped to lift her teacup, her pinky sticking out like she was trying to shake something off it. "You know that *I* will give Hattie the best care."

How could she know what was best for me? She didn't even know me. Trouble is, Pa thought it was best too, or I wouldn't be here. "You got the gift for learning, Hattie Belle, and your grandma will get you a good education," Pa had said. "Guess she's your only kin now, other than me. It'd be a shame if you never got acquainted or saw where your ma grew up."

I consoled myself by thinking how Grandmother couldn't be frost through and through, because Ma got lonesome for her, same as I got lonesome for my ma. But now my ma was buried under the plum tree by our little cabin back home in the hills above Pepacton, where I was born. Now all I had left of her was Grandmother. I should've been grateful just to meet her finally, but for the time being it was a sentiment I couldn't muster.

I walked back up to the house and waited for Grandmother to tell me what to do next. Hortensia Holmes Greymoor was her proper name, which made a hollow windy sound in my mouth. She was a chinless gray bird with a small, beakish nose, warbly throat, and little eyes with droopy skin around them. Her hair wisped like feathers, and a few straggly ones sprouted from a tiny cheek mole. She didn't look like my ma, who was lovely.

It was hard to keep my lip from trembling. I wanted to go off somewhere alone and kick something or sob until I was completely wrung out. I thought I needed to do that before I could get on with things here.

Grandmother gave me an anxious look. "Dear, dear . . ." she said, fingering the lace of her lavender brocade and then humming in a bewildered sort of way.

At least there was one good thing about her. She didn't look like me. I was tall for my age and scrawny to boot, with chopped-off hair (my fault) and a strong chin like a boy's even though I was eleven and plenty old enough to have girl looks. I got a shuddery feeling just thinking about that and instead concentrated on how improved I looked in my blue checked dress that matched my eyes and my hair grown long enough to tickle the middle of my neck.

"I've got a strong constitution," I said. "But if I don't pee real soon, it might get busted."

That cracked the ice some. Grandmother sucked in air like she'd been socked in the belly. "Of all the . . . uncouth . . . uncivilized . . ." she sputtered. I didn't know what she meant exactly, but I could tell it was a cold, unkind thing to say.

She grabbed my hand and took off on a trot into the house, through the dark drawing room with the drapes closed, through the dark dining room with the drapes closed, down a long, dark hallway with the doors closed, around a sharp corner, down several steps and across a landing before she stopped. "In there," she said, pointing to a door. "The closet where you . . . you relieve yourself," she said quickly, her cheeks getting pink. But she still clung to my hand.

"Um . . ." I said, jiggling and shifting from foot to foot,

"I'm pretty sure I can manage by myself from here, Grandmother."

"Why, of course you can, dear. I never thought otherwise," she said in shocked surprise.

I tugged gently, trying to pull my hand free from her grasp.

"Oh, dear. Whatever was I thinking?" She dropped my hand and gently brushed her palm against a fold in her dress. "Take your time, dear. No rush, dear," she said. "Just follow the corridor back when you're ready. I'll show you where to wash properly then."

"Dear," I said under my breath. It really was a closet, and the only way to get in was to turn around, back in, hitch up your things, and sit down. Once the door was shut, it was dark. I mean dark, as in bumping into a black bear on an inky, moonless night.

I did not have a warm feeling about Grandmother, and it was plain enough that she disapproved of Pa and me.

When I came out, Grandmother had disappeared. At least I was alone for a few minutes, but my tears were swollen up the size of a goose egg and stuck sideways in my throat and wouldn't budge. There were the stairs going back the way we'd come, but there were two doors on this landing, too. The first one wasn't locked, so I eased it open. Wooden steps led down through a dusky darkness to a pool of light at the bottom, while a musty, dead air smell came up. I took a few steps down, and the light brightened to a soft brown. I hurried to the bottom of the steps and stopped in a shaft of light speckled with motes of dust, shining in through the square of a little window. I looked around.

Sturdy brick arches, like bridges, spanned the whole width of the house, as if there might have been a river here once. It wasn't scary down here, just hugely empty and silent. I walked from end to end, leaving behind telltale footprints in the powdery brown dust of the floor, my steps soft and muffled like walking in snow. There was nothing here but cobwebs and one wall of shelves filled with crocks and jars.

I walked to the far end of the cellar again and leaned my forehead against the cool bricks. Down here, I could scream and cry and maybe they wouldn't hear me. My eyes burned, and I felt sick all over. Uncouth, she called me. Brushed her hand off like I had warts or vermin. I kicked the backside of a brick arch. "I don't care if she is kin. I don't want to be here," I muttered. *Kick.* "I want to go home." *Kick.* "I want my pa." *Kick.* The sobs started to come. *Kick. Kick. Kick.*

To my horror, one of the bricks gave way and fell to the floor. I gasped. I hadn't been here more than an hour and I'd broken something already.

I wiped my tears and bent to put the brick back in line with the rest. It slipped into place easily, as though it had been loose already. I pulled the brick back out and peeked into its hole. A bit of cloth was showing in the weak light. I stuck my hand in and pulled out a small bundle. It was a dirty linen napkin wrapped around what felt like spokes and points and a wheel.

I unfolded the napkin and at first giggled nervously at what lay in my hand. It was only three tarnished silver spoons, four forks, and a pocket watch with *WEG* engraved in fancy letters like some sort of code. I pushed the catch, and the cover of the watch snapped open. The glass face was cracked and one of the hands had fallen off. I tried winding it, but nothing happened. I shook it, and the broken springs and pieces rattled inside.

Now I felt a prickle go up my spine. It didn't make sense to hide silverware. It was a queer thing to do, queer and creepy. Suddenly spooked, I shoved the bundle back into the hole and set the brick in place. I scurried up the stairs, my heart fluttering wildly with the shivery feeling that something was after me.

There was no one around on the other side of the door, and no one was calling for me. I opened the third door on the landing. There was a short hallway with another door. Maybe this one was the way outside. I went over and slowly turned the knob, but before I could push against the door, it was yanked open, and I fell into the kitchen and a nightmare of black.

"Been sneaking around and snooping already, have we?" The cook who had served us tea was glaring down at me suspiciously. "Don't think I didn't hear you out there," she said, flapping her arms. Her name was Rose, but the only thing rosy about her was her red face. She wore all black and looked like a turkey buzzard.

"Wasn't sneaking," I said. "Just having a look."

"*Hmpf.* More than a look, I'd say. Don't think I can't see the dust on your boots," she said. "I've seen your kind before. Breaker, that's what." She stumped back to a thick wooden table and picked up a cleaver. *Wamp!* She smacked it hard through a whole chicken. "Everything here is breakable. Got that? You break something valuable here, and I'll make you real sorry for it. That's a promise you can count on." *Wamp* went her cleaver again. "And another thing—nothing had better go missing or I'll know who's the guilty party."

All I could do was stare. She couldn't possibly be the wonderful Rose Ma talked about. Patient Rose. Understanding Rose. Clever and gentle Rose, who taught Ma how to make gingerbread men and sweet plum pie with a flaky crust. This Rose was a thorny old buzzard who made no bones about not liking me or wanting me here.

Buzzard Rose scowled and glared at me from beneath hooded eyes. "Not much like your mother, are you? She was no sneak. Never intended to break anything either. I never minded having our Lily hanging around or helping out." Rose's face softened when she said Ma's name.

I edged toward the table, where Rose was chopping and flouring the chicken pieces. "I was hoping you'd tell me about her," I said softly.

*Whack!* Off with a chicken leg. "I already did," Rose said. "Said you ain't like her; you're like *him*. You ain't much like a girl at all."

"Aren't," I snapped. "Besides, I know that already."

"Hmm." *Whack! Whack!*

*Old Buzzard.* I studied Rose for a minute longer. Nope. There wasn't one good thing about her. I backed toward the door, slipped out, and traipsed up the hall, trying the other closed doors, but they were all locked.

When I walked through the dining room, I noticed dark spots on the wallpaper where pictures or furniture used to be. There was definitely something queer about this house.

A rush of relief washed over me when I found Grandmother in the drawing room. Even if she didn't know what to say or do, or how to act natural around me, even if she was unkind to me and cold to Pa, she felt pretty safe compared to everything else. And she smelled like lilacs.

# CHAPTER TWO

I sat hidden on the wide windowsill behind the drapes in my room and thought about Ma. Best were Ma's sweet smiles and her enchanting pretends, like collecting magical wishes in our aprons at dewtime and searching for fairy houses where the deep purple violets grew and the wind shushed in the hemlocks. Like leaving gifts for the fairies—tiny star and half-moon cookies, loaves the size of thumbnails, cloaks smaller than our little fingers. Ma loved all the invisible and gentle beings. But now she was dead, and there was no sign that she had been a child in this dusty house with fussy old ladies.

*Lily. Lily. Lily.* It was odd hearing people say her real name. Pa called her Ma, same as me. My Lily, Grandmother calls her. Our Lily, the old Buzzard says. Ma's name feels like water, sounds like music on my tongue. *Lily.*

I'd been here one sorrowfully long rainy week and sorely needed to write down a few good reasons to be in Kingston (because so far, I could only think of the reasons *not* to stay here).

*1. Pa thinks it's a good thing.*

*2. I get to see where Ma lived and learn more about her.* I can think of Lovely Lily sipping lemonade and reading Longfellow in a house filled with light. The light is gone, but the pretty flower gardens she loved are still here.

*3. I've gotten to meet Lily's mother, Hortensia the Unkind.* That's done and crossed off.

*4. I don't have to do any more cooking. No more burned biscuits and gravy like paste, or scorched potatoes.* Buzzard Rose is a good cook, I'll give her that. But there's nothing else good about her, and nothing can make me say so.

*5. I'm supposed to be getting a good education.* I'm puzzled about that one. Grandmother hasn't said one thing about my going to school.

*6. I'm sleeping in a real bed that is soft and plump.* I hate to let on, even to myself, that it's grand to have a pretty room all my own instead of a windowless loft where we stored burlap bags of nuts and hung ropes of onions to dry. Ma said her room here was a lovely shade of violet, and I know it must be one of the four that's locked up on this floor. Mine is green, which makes me think of the pines and hemlocks and balsams, like being in our little cabin in the woods.

I was terrible homesick for Pa. Used to be we were ornery cusses to each other after Ma died, 'cause when she died, she took the sun and the moon and every drop of sweetness from our lives. Our natural meanness just took over, grew wild as a briar patch, choked out any fondness he and I might have had for a while. Pa had me wear overalls, like a boy. Called me a boy, too. Took a long time working with him in the woods, and our fearful but wonderful trip down the river on a log raft, to learn all over again that Pa did love me, that I was no boy to him, that I was his girl, his own Hattie Belle. Maybe, like he said, it *was* best for me to be here with Grandmother, but it didn't *feel* best.

What would feel best now would be Pa and me and

his good laughter, his jokes and songs, and the way he whistled like a hawk to let me know he was almost home. Best now would be knowing that Pa and Jasper were waiting for me to come back. Right now, I should be on a raft flying down the river with them. If I closed my eyes, I could almost see Jasper's warm brown eyes and big grin. I could almost hear him telling me again about how we'd go fishing for brook trout in one of the hollows, how he'd teach me to catch them in my hands and to coax a woodchuck to eat from my fingers, and maybe tame a crow for a pet, if I wanted.

Now Pa and Jasper were clear on the other side of the Catskill mountain range. Pa said it was farther than a hawk whistle would carry, but not that far away if you knew the old Indian paths and trails blazed by the first settlers. Which meant that I'd just have to wait for him to come and fetch me.

I wiped my cheeks and read back over the good reasons to be here.

OK, six reasons was a good start. Then I saw that maybe there were seven reasons to stay in Kingston, because from my window I spied a roundish girl with long yellow curls about my age. She was bouncing a ball on the walk of the blue house next door—a house even larger than Grandmother's. The blue house had a tall front tower and sparkling white gingerbread that looked good enough to eat. The folk over there had their own horse and carriage and a barn to keep them in.

I flew out of my room and pounded down the stairs, though I had been admonished to walk sedately at all times. "Grandmother, there's a girl outside," I said breathlessly. "I'm going out to talk to her."

Grandmother looked thoughtful and nervously patted the brooch that fastened her lace collar. "Give yourself a little more time, Hattie Belle. It might prove beneficial to observe that child a little longer."

I gave her a dark, hooded look like the one Rose wore and edged toward the door. I knew she thought Pa and me were uncouth, not good enough for city folks and city ways. "I know how to mind my manners," I said.

She raised her eyebrows and tucked her lips out of sight. "Fine then, Hattie Belle, as you wish, but do consider wearing your hat, and do mind your words, dear."

I sucked in my breath and brushed my hand over my hair. It was getting nearly long enough to braid again, but it still looked like boy hair. I started to thank her, but I pressed my lips together and rushed to the hall tree. I grabbed my hat, squashed it over the evidence of my folly, and hurried out the door.

"Tea in the library when you return," she called as I went out.

I didn't answer, just banged the door shut with a good loud crack even though it was against the rules. At last, after seven rainy days of being stuck inside, I was out. I was sick of being told not to say *pee* or *swig* or *arse* and a potful of other words not good enough unless they were dressed up fancy, pretending to be something finer. I was sick of learning to use forks and spoons in silly sizes for different foods when just one of each was plenty good enough. We even swept crumbs from the tablecloth with a silver dustpan and brush. My friend Jasper would never believe that. I was told in a shocked voice by Grandmother that I was not to use it as a plaything and it was never to be used to sweep up crumbs beneath the table.

I was scolded for putting elbows on the table, swinging my feet against chair legs, and speaking with so much as a crumb in my mouth. I could not stare or point, even indoors, and absolutely no farting was allowed, even if I called it breaking wind and apologized for the smell. No thumping was allowed on the stairs, no running up and down the long corridors or cupping my hands and hollering out to hear the echo come back.

I was not allowed out of the yard or even off the brick walks if the grass was wet. But so far I hadn't gone anywhere because of the rain, and neither Grandmother nor Rose had gone out, because pretty near everything a body could ask for was delivered to the house. For seven long days I learned manners that Ma never told me about, but mostly I practiced sitting still and being quiet, watched Grandmother worry her cuffs and collar, and listened to her *Dear me* to death with don'ts.

Finally, I was out of the house away from them and on my own with the warm sunshine and fresh air. *Free!* I raced around to the side lawn, fearful that the blue house girl had disappeared. She hadn't. I slowed when I got to the black iron fence with spikes on top that marched all the way around the house and met at a gate. It seemed to say "keep out" to anyone who did not have a special invitation.

I marched back and forth in the wet grass, waiting for that girl to notice me. I cautiously glanced her way, and she saw me all right between bounces of that ball, but she didn't make a move to come over to the fence. Finally, I stopped. "Hello," I called, tilting my head so I

17

could see with both eyes through the space between the black spears. When I did, my hat fell off and landed on the ground. She perked right up, her face all curious. She scurried over to the bars like a squirrel after a nut before I could grab my hat and clamp it back on my head.

"Are you a boy or a girl?" she asked breathlessly.

"A girl, same as you," I said. "I'm Hattie Belle Basket, and I've come to live with my grandmother. Pleased to make your acquaintance."

Up close she was not so pretty. She had a round, flat face with little piggy eyes and a stuck-up nose, but she had the loveliest yellow curls that bounced when she walked, and bobbed when she moved her head, and boinged when she patted them, which she did pretty regular.

"I'm Ivy Victoria—after the queen of England—Blackmore Vandermeer," she said in a superior, knowing way. "You may be a girl, but I think you should know that you look like a boy. Why is your hair so short?"

Right then and there, I knew that I wasn't going to like her or her curls. I did not have that nice, warm feeling like when I'd met Jasper. "None of your business," I said.

"Your face is dark like an Indian's," she said. "Are you a savage?"

I opened my mouth to deny it, to tell her I was sun-burned and browned from working like an ox in the woods and riding down the river on a raft, but what came out was something else. "Yup," I said. "Injun." Guess those yellow curls made me want to scalp her. Didn't intend to lie, but that's how it turned out.

"You talk funny too. Did you know that?" she said.

"I talk with my mouth, same as you," I said.

"I mean, you sound like a country bumpkin. Do you know what that means?" She spoke slowly like I was ignorant or something worse.

I nodded. Yup, I was pretty sure that was like being called a Hill Hawk and uncouth. I grabbed my hat off the ground and pushed it on my head.

She got a sneaky look then. "You might be fun to play games with," she said. "Come over here now."

"Can't," I said. I was not about to take orders from the bossy likes of her. "My grandmother is waiting for me."

"Please?" she said in a pleading sort of way. "I'll let you play with my ball."

I wet my lips. I wanted to bounce that ball, all right. Maybe she just wanted a friend.

But then she pressed her face up against the fence. "Why doesn't your grandmother wear black?" she said.

A cold chill went down my spine. "Why should she?" I asked.

"I'll be glad to tell you if you come over here."

She still had a sneaky look. "Nope," I said, shaking my head. I turned and started walking back to the house.

"Hattie Belle," she said. "You'd better come over here tomorrow or you'll be sorry."

I was sorry already. Real sorry I hadn't listened to Grandmother. Real sorry, because in the low-down sinking feeling crawling along the bottom of my stomach, I knew I was stuck with the blue house girl. And that made two people I didn't trust and three people that I was uneasy with, and one more reason to fly away home. If I could.

# CHAPTER THREE

With a sorry sag to my shoulders, I hung up my hat and studied myself in the mirror of the hall tree. I was a sorry-looking girl, all right. Ma said I would be lovely one day. But not today. Pretty sure it wouldn't be tomorrow or even next month. Right now my failure was written all over my scrawny self like chalk on a slate board, written so big that Grandmother would see it for sure.

I didn't mind going to the library, though. It was the best room in the house and the only room that didn't seem to be missing pieces of anything. There were shelves of darkly bound books, deep, heavily cushioned chairs with soft pillows and knitted throws, low tables for setting tea and books, a writing desk, a clock on the wall and a clock on the mantel that never ticked, kerosene lamps with light glowing through green shades or rose-colored globes, a dark-patterned rug over a wood floor, and a fireplace that used gas and heated the room on damp, chilly days. No wood to chop here. I could add that to my list of good reasons to be in Kingston in place of Ivy Victoria, who might have been reason number seven but never would be now.

When I went in, Grandmother was sitting on the chaise lounge reading a book. Soft light fell across her lap. The tea tray was placed on the table beside her. "There you are," she said, looking up as soon as my footfalls clattered on the wooden floor. In a flash, her eyes swept over me and she saw exactly how my meeting went. "I'll just pour the tea now. Rose has made us some wonderful little cakes," she said.

I sat down in the chair across from Grandmother. "Well . . . I met the blue house girl," I said.

"And?"

"She said her name was Ivy Victoria—after the queen of England—Blackmore Vandermeer."

"I see. It was like that, was it?"

"Yup," I said glumly. "She says I have to come over tomorrow or I'll be sorry."

"Oh, dear," Grandmother said, worrying her cuffs again.

"She can't make me."

Grandmother raised her eyebrows. "It's not that simple, dear. This is hardly the woods. There's a certain protocol of genteel society that needs to be observed. You did make the first overture; you are obliged to follow through."

"But I am from the woods, so why should I?" I scoffed.

"Would you want that child to think you cowardly?"

Grandmother was smart about that. I shook my head, not caring one bit to hear her priggish little sniff.

"Have your tea. Tomorrow is soon enough to worry about the Vandermeer child."

Couldn't help wondering if Ma had ever known a meddlesome girl like Ivy. I waited, hoping Grandmother might say something about my ma when she was a girl. So far, we had done more looking off at corners than any friendly talking, so I wasn't finding out much. And, remembering Ivy's question about wearing black, I wanted to know why Ma had never talked about Grandfather when it was hard for me now not to bust out bragging on my Pa.

"My pa can pretty near walk on water," I said. "He's the best steersman on the whole river, knows every rift and island and the way to maneuver them. Everybody says so. Everybody says Amos Basket is the best."

Guess she didn't care for that, 'cause she started to talk about her own pa like he was the king of a whole continent. "My father, your great-grandfather," she said, "was a successful merchant with a fleet of dayliners, a captain of the river. He built this house for me as my dowry. Everything seemed so easy in those years when my father was still alive. Now the family has a few day-liners—nothing opulent, just boats, really—that carry passengers from town to town along the Hudson. We've nothing like the fortune my father made." She was all friendly about it, and I didn't mind learning about my great-grandfather; he sounded real adventurous, sort of like Pa and me.

Grandmother still didn't mention her own husband, my grandfather, just like Ma never had, so I said extra sweet-like, "Tell me about my grandfather. Was he a riverboat captain?"

Grandmother grew a little pale; her fingers shook, and

her cup clinked against the saucer. "Your grandfather came from a good family. When he was young, he did a great many things well," she said. "When our Lily was small, he'd get down on the floor on all fours and play horse with her, give her jolly rides on his back and make her giggle. He surprised her with trinkets and baubles, colorful things that would catch a child's eye, and he told her about little people. . . ." Grandmother broke off and gazed at a corner.

"Sort of like pretends?" I asked.

Grandmother opened her mouth, then closed it. She shook her head. "Your grandfather was fragile, Hattie, dear. . . . He had troubles with business and troubles of a different nature." She looked sad, bowed her head.

"Guess he died, huh?" I offered in a softer tone.

Grandmother sort of nodded but did not say a word about it. That seemed strange. Dead was dead, no denying it. I picked up a small cake and nibbled at it, thinking about this. "Ma was delicate—fragile-like," I said. "Was Grandfather like that?"

"Somewhat, but different," she said, thoughtfully pressing fingers against her lips. She nodded and moved her fingers to her lace collar. "Yes . . . quite different."

*Good.* I didn't want Ma to be like him, because even if

Grandmother didn't say it, I still knew that he cast a shadow over Ma, over Grandmother too. He felt like a shadow now, lurking just outside the light cast from the lamps. Talking about Grandfather gave me a cold feeling of something not right.

Grandmother took a bite of cake and dabbed at her lips with her napkin. "My father loved clocks," she said. "And books and stories. He told the most wonderful stories about the river, ghost stories, legends."

I was real interested in the part about ghosts, but I didn't let on. I sipped my tea and looked out over the rim of my little cup, studying her. It was important to keep focused on the things Grandmother glossed over. "I was wondering about the clocks," I said. "Why don't they tick?"

Grandmother gave me a thoughtful look. "They would run, but the keys are lost or mislaid somewhere. I've looked everywhere, but . . ." Grandmother got a faraway look.

"Maybe I could find them," I said, gazing about the room. Keys might be anywhere. Fallen behind books or dropped without notice and kicked under furniture.

"Not today, dear," she said, which I had to admit was a relief. I didn't fancy stumbling across more queer bundles.

"Wouldn't Great-Grandfather want his clocks to run?" I asked.

Grandmother blinked and looked misty eyed. "Finish your tea," she said sharply. But she didn't answer my question. Slick as anything, she just moved on to something else. That was worth remembering—*changing your talk to suit your own self.* I saw that there might be endless possibilities for future use. "After you've finished, I'll read to you," she said brightly, which I figured was a clever way to make me sit still and be quiet.

When Grandmother read, her voice was true and strong, and she read with great expression and changed her voice for each of the March sisters—Meg, Jo, Beth, and Amy. Guess I was a lot like Jo—boyish and long and prone to using slang words that weren't always proper.

Grandmother lulled me into a storybook world with her voice, but I didn't forget how she really felt about me and Pa and our ways. Grandmother wasn't sweet or lovely like Ma. Still, when she read, there was a deliciousness about her, like the tempting smell of a meat pie straight from the oven.

I moved to sit next to her on the lounge. At first, I felt a little stiff. Had she read this way to Ma—little Lily—in the good days before things had gone wrong? I didn't ask, but I felt pretty sure about it.

If she thought we were on the same side together, she might share the shadowy secrets of Grandfather, and why the keys had gone missing and the silver was squirreled away, and why she didn't wear black, and where all the furniture and pictures had gone, and why she had hurried Pa away, and mostly, why Ma had run off and never come back. It was a powerful lot to find out. And that's why I had to stay here and behave properly, though sitting so close to Grandmother made me even more lonesome for Pa and Jasper and my real home.

# CHAPTER FOUR

The next morning at breakfast, I temporarily forgot about Ivy Victoria, because Grandmother said a tutor was coming to be interviewed.

"A tutor?" I fumed quietly, eyeing her suspiciously. It wasn't fair to bring the schooling to me. It made me a prisoner, nearly. "Mother taught me a little Latin and some biology, and I went to school more regular than anybody, except when the weather was bad. I'm a good scholar, Grandmother. I can cipher in my head. Skipped me some grades, too," I said.

"Fine, Hattie Belle," she said. "But school is different here."

Better is what she meant.

"You have potential, I believe, but I need to assess what you've learned and bring you up to your grade level in all subject matter with the hopes of getting you into the Academy. There are many fine schools here, but it's the best one in Kingston and one of the best in the whole country."

I perked up. The tutor was only temporary. I smiled and spread my napkin neatly across my lap and spooned some currant jelly onto my biscuit and winked at the egg cup in front of me. The jiggly half-boiled egg made me think of a rheumy eyeball, and I was relieved when it didn't wink back. "Grandmother," I said. "Wouldn't it be simpler if I went to a regular school like before?" At least it would give me a chance to make some real friends instead of being stuck with the blue house girl.

"Simpler, perhaps," she said. "But do give the tutor a try. Everyone deserves at least a chance. Don't you think?"

I clamped my teeth together real hard.

Buzzard Rose came in carrying an envelope. "Found

this dropped through the letter slot, Hortensia. It's addressed to the miss."

"Is it from Pa?" I asked hopefully. Maybe he'd changed his mind. Maybe he was coming to take me back home.

Grandmother shook her head and passed it over to me.

I smelled the powdery roses even before I touched the envelope, and I got that low-down miserable feeling crawling along the bottom of my stomach again. The note said that my presence was requested for tea with Ivy Victoria at two o'clock. A servant would call for me. "Can we pretend it didn't come?" I asked woefully.

Grandmother shook her head again.

Rose sat down in the chair across the table from me and looked smug. "Ivy Victoria," she said, smacking her lips deliciously.

"She said I looked like a boy."

Rose smirked her agreement.

"I'll put some curl in your hair," Grandmother said. "I'll arrange it so it appears longer. You'll be fine; don't worry." But it was plain to me she was plenty worried by the way she fingered her brooch.

"She's an awful bossy and suspicious sort," I said. "She asked me why you don't wear black, Grandmother."

Grandmother went pale, and Rose's red face grew purple in alarm. So . . . Ivy Victoria had touched on something real important. I was curious about what, all right.

"It wouldn't hurt this one time, Hortensia, if she didn't go," Buzzard Rose said. "There's no time to see about everything today. We've enough to tend to without trying to turn the miss into a young lady. She's got too much of the other one in her."

"Yesss," Grandmother said, still looking rattled. "But you really must make the best of it, Hattie, dear. You may get on with her after a fashion." But her voice wasn't convincing. None of us believed I would get on with her at all.

"I'll try," I said.

"Try what?" muttered Rose.

"Now, Rose," Grandmother said in warning. "She's Lily's child."

"Our Lily," Rose said, her face softening.

"Yes, our Lily," Grandmother said, "and our Hattie Belle."

Thorny old Rose nodded, but there was no give in her. I saw that by her narrowed eyes and grim face. Guess Rose didn't think I was good enough for Ma. I wanted to spit out that Ma always said that there wasn't anything finer than having me and Pa to love her. That would show the old buzzard. Instead I acted sweet. "Why don't I help Rose clean up the breakfast things, Grandmother?" I said, knowing how the old buzzard would feel about that. "I'd like to help."

Rose came right out of her chair. "I can manage fine by myself," she blustered. Hurriedly, she began to clear the table.

"We'll tidy the drawing room, Hattie, before the young gentleman tutor arrives."

Already the day had taken some crooked turns—tea with Ivy Victoria and the tutor coming up from New York. But Grandmother and Rose getting fearfully alarmed about what Ivy had told me led me to suspect that I'd stumbled onto yet another creepy secret.

# CHAPTER FIVE

The tutor was late, and his mackintosh dripped a flood all over the front hall because he had forgotten to bring an umbrella. He looked interesting and pleasant enough, though a bit rumpled. And hungry.

He took his tea with four lumps of sugar and milk to the brim. He drank three cups and devoured the biscuits left over from breakfast. The way he ate reminded me of Jasper, but the tutor was tall and thin and smoothly pale, like a flagpole painted white. His eyes were smoke-colored and gently doelike, and his shaggy black hair, longer than mine, curled down into his neck and brushed his shoulders. He had wiry hairs sprouting from his chin, which he fingered nervously when he wasn't sipping or munching.

I eyed the tutor. He looked weak and woebegone. He looked like he was running away from something. His name was Horace Bottle, and he had been a student at university in New York. He had discontinued studies for a time, he said, because of a long illness—scarlet fever—and lack of funds. His physician had suggested he seek a tutoring position, something that wouldn't require a great deal of excitement or physical exertion, a way to get back on his feet.

Grandmother only nodded and continued to study him. She seemed to see something about him that I couldn't. She looked over his letters of reference and then asked me to give Rose a hand in the kitchen.

I didn't want to leave. The tutor was much too interesting, and it gave me the giggles, nearly, to watch him press a finger into the crumbs dotted on his plate and lick them off while looking for more. I did hope to stay and hear what Grandmother had to say. "Shall I clear the tea things, Grandmother?" I asked.

"Leave them for now," she said.

Guess she was in a hurry to get rid of Horace Bottle. I

felt a little sorry for him about that. Because he looked so forlorn, I gave him a smile. For a second, he looked surprised. Then he smiled back, and it made him seem like a different person. Not desperate. Not weak. Lost, maybe. Lonely. I got a feeling about him, not like the nice warm feeling of meeting Jasper, but good. A good feeling. I trotted off to the kitchen feeling hopeful about making friends with the tutor.

Buzzard Rose was up to her elbows in flour and dough. She scowled and cast me a dour look. I decided to be real cheerful just to vex her.

"Grandmother said I should help you," I said, giving her a wide, toothy grin.

Rose raised her eyebrows. "*Hmpf.* What's made you so mannerly all of a sudden? Up to something, are we?" She pulled her eyebrows back down and started to knead the dough.

"Yup," I said. "Up to no good. Sneaking around probably, snooping."

"Something fishy all right," Rose said, but she sounded puzzled, like maybe she was wrong about that.

I tucked that bit away to use again: *When you're accused of something, do not deny the truth, especially if the truth is what you want taken as a lie.*

Rose sighed. "As long as you're hanging around, guess you could sweep up the floor when I'm done. 'Course, your mother never had to be asked. When she wasn't any bigger than a mouse hardly, she'd drag that stool over from the corner there and stand on it to sift the flour for me. Always real careful, our Lily."

"She made great pretends when she baked bread and cookies," I said. "Did you teach her about pretends, Rose? About how the flour changed and became magical when it went through the sifter? Was it you?"

"Pretends? Whatever do you mean?" Rose said, casting me a worried look.

"You know, Rose. Fairy dust, angel dust that sparkled," I said coaxingly. But then, last fall there had been a couple of times when Ma thought the flour had changed into tiny flying bugs, and she had covered her face and wept. But there were no bugs; it was only flour, white and powdery and harmless.

"No, don't know anything about pretends or magic," Rose said. "Lily was a quiet, well-mannered child. She was the only angel around here."

I nodded, hoping Rose would go on.

"Did she miss us, our Lily?" Rose blurted out.

Didn't care to be soft to Buzzard Rose, but the only

37

other choice was to lie. "Yup," I said. "Guess she did all right." I hung my head and silently cussed myself out.

"Knew it," Rose said, sounding smug. "I always knew Lily wanted to come back."

"Never said she wanted to come back," I said hotly. Rose's head snapped up, like she'd been cuffed. She narrowed her eyes. "You impertinent little mongrel." Rose muttered and turned back to her kneading. "I'll sweep my own floor."

I went over and stood next to her. "If being a mongrel means being like my pa, then I'm proud to be one," I whispered. Then I poked a hole in her bread dough and ducked away before she could swat me. *Thorny Old Buzzard.*

I heard the front door bang. I rushed out into the hall and saw the back of Horace Bottle going down the walk.

"You sent him away," I accused Grandmother. "Thought you said everybody deserved a chance."

Grandmother flushed and smoothed her lace cuffs. "He's only gone off to collect the rest of his things and to make some purchases. Despite his appetite, he'll do fine for us, Hattie Belle."

Rose was right. I was impertinent. Ma would want me to say I was sorry to Grandmother, but the sorry words were stuck deep down, hiding in the dark like cowards. I stared down at the water spots on the wood floor where Horace Bottle had dripped. "Should I wipe up the floor, Grandmother?" I asked, which was as close to sorry as I could get for her at the moment.

Grandmother smiled. "You and I must open up a couple of rooms. Then we'll see about those curls."

Curls for tea, she meant. I'd been so wicked to Rose that I figured I deserved whatever bossy games Ivy Victoria Blackmore Vandermeer had planned for me. But I'd worry about that later. Right now, Grandmother was going to give me a look at what was behind some of those locked doors. Maybe I'd find out more about Ma or something about the secrets here.

# CHAPTER SIX

Grandmother and I donned caps and aprons left over from the old days of maids and climbed the stairs to the top of the house armed with feather dusters and dry mops, brush and broom, polish and rags. The third-story stairs were steep and narrow and thick with dust. I had stood at the bottom peering up into the faint light more than once but never ventured up. I would have been caught by my bootprints. Then Rose would act like I was a no-count criminal loose in Hortensia's house and keep her buzzardy eyes on my every move.

The tutor's rooms were to be at the top of the house, and with no hesitation, Grandmother kicked a door open.

"It wasn't even locked," I spluttered, surprised by this and by her sudden unlady-like behavior. If this door wasn't locked, maybe the one across the hall wasn't either. I knew the ones on the floors below were: I had tried them all more than once, hoping to find Ma's violet room.

"Oh, no, no reason for it to be," Grandmother said cheerfully.

Waves of disappointment washed over me, because there really was no reason to lock this door. There was nothing here except a thick coating of dust on spindly stick furniture. Dead flies looked like spilled raisins on the sills and floors; pale, thin spiders scuttled away into the corners of their webs at our approach. There was nothing that hinted of Ma, but still it was a private place removed from the goings-on of the rest of the house—a small bedroom with a window seat in one of the gables, a small adjoining sitting room with built-in bookcases, and a schoolroom, all back to back like railroad cars. I would gladly trade places with skinny Mr. Bottle.

"All this for the tutor?" I exclaimed. "Are the rooms on the other side of the passage like this?" I asked hopefully.

Grandmother shook her head. "The other side was the servants' quarters at one time. Nothing of interest there," she said hastily.

Too hastily, I thought. There might be something over there, things that had belonged to Ma or maybe valuables that Rose was worried I'd break.

We were busy then with mops and feather dusters, rags and polish, and putting fresh bedding on the narrow bed, and it was all a frolic. I liked the bustle of cleaning. How easy it seemed after swinging a mallet or pulling on a long oar in a windy, rushing river.

"We'll cozy it up with some pillows and bring in some lamps and a fresh pitcher of water later on," Grandmother said with a weary sigh when the rooms were done.

It was the first I noticed Grandmother looking worn out, and the first I'd given a thought to how much trouble and work I was making for her. I mean, the tutor was here just for me. "Yet another person to feed and lodge," according to Rose, but meaning me as much as the tutor. I was trying to be proper, but I still slammed doors and thumped down the stairs and fidgeted awful at meals and picked at my food.

Grandmother sighed again. "Enough of being Cinderella," she said, yanking off her cap and blowing her nose on a handkerchief she pulled from the waistband of her apron. "It's time to get you ready for the ball."

"The ball?" I asked.

"Yes, tea with Ivy Victoria, after the queen of England," Grandmother said, raising her eyebrows. "Quite a challenge for your day."

"Yup," I muttered, remembering that Ivy thought I was an Indian and she would probably ask me all about that. What did I know about Indians? "The Song of Hiawatha," the wigwam of Nokomis, and the shores of Gitche Gumee. I gave a nervous giggle. More lies I'd be telling.

"What do you know about the Vandermeers?" I asked Grandmother as we started down the passage. I bumped against the door on the other side, thumped it hard with the broom handle too. Didn't budge. Drat.

"What would you like to know?" Grandmother asked, ignoring my bumbling.

"Don't know," I offered feebly. There were too many rules of conversation that I needed to learn. Up until I had come here, I'd chattered on like a chipmunk, never thinking much about what I was saying. Grandmother listened, but she always turned the talk in another direction. Made me feel like a horse with a bit and bridle and Grandmother holding the reins—"Gee up! Whoa!" And a good yank to turn me about and keep control. Made me start to think more and chatter a whole lot less.

We trooped down to the kitchen and the savory smell of bread baking in the black oven and the comforting warmth of the stove after the damp chill of the third floor. If only Rose weren't so hateful, the kitchen would be a favored place.

Rose had curling tongs heating on the stove. I pressed my lips together and squeezed my eyes shut and scarcely breathed when Grandmother crimped my papered locks of hair. I couldn't do with any more damage to my already sorry looks.

Grandmother paid very close attention to what she was doing, and I soon had a cap of curls that danced when I shook them. I didn't have to see to know that my hair was much improved. I could tell by the pleased look on Grandmother's face, and even Rose brightened when I turned to face her, looked at me like I was a different sort of child and not a mongrel from the backwoods.

"A bow, ma'am, at the back of her head, would give her the look of a young lady," Rose said agreeably. Hah! Rose was just saying it to please Grandmother.

"Why, Rose, just the thing," Grandmother said.

I ran to peer in the hall mirror to see how I looked. Different, all right. More like a girl, but nothing like Ma. I moved closer to my reflection and patted my curls. Then I saw it. My eyes were blue like Pa's, but rounder, larger like Ma's. It was a small thing, but it made me breathe quite fast in little gasps like I was seeing a real girl for once.

The change didn't last long. By the time we'd gotten the tutor settled and the Vandermeer's servant came round to call, my hair was limp and sorry, and the bow fell out.

I went out into the dismal, pouring rain with the manservant from next door holding an umbrella over my head with a gloved hand. My list of good reasons to stay in Kingston was not getting any longer.

# CHAPTER SEVEN

I walked the short distance to the Vandermeers' thinking hard about Indians and my sorry hair. I decided that Molting Hawk would make a good name for my looks. Woefully, I decided that it'd be better if I claimed not to know anything of my Indian kin, which would be the truth, though I might frighten Ivy with one or two scary lies. Cheering myself with the prospect of a scalping or kidnapping story, I decided tea might turn into a frolic after all, until I stepped inside the door being held for me by the servant.

That hall was all dark, carved wood with a bright chandelier, prisms dancing from the wind gusting in, scattering the light and making rainbows and shadows on the ceilings and walls. The Vandermeers' patterned rugs were plush, their wallpaper vivid. Nothing here was faded or dull. The rooms I could peek at from the hall entry were filled with so much stuff that it blurred together in a jumble as if they intended to set up a department store like the Bloomingdale's one in New York, where Pa had taken me to buy my dress.

Ivy Victoria came bouncing down the stairs with her perfect fat-sausage curls, rosy cheeks, and a pinkish patterned dress, a different dress from the day before. She grabbed my hand like we were old chums and pulled me toward the stairs. "Tea in the nursery," she said. "I've asked Mother to leave us alone."

Before I could feel relieved about that, she went on. "Of course they would leave me alone, but they won't leave *us* alone. Everyone is anxious to learn about you."

"Because I'm part Indian," I said.

"No," she said, and lowered her voice. "It's because you're Lily Greymoor's daughter that they care a thing about you at all. Mother says there's quite a stir about you."

I didn't much like being a stir. Didn't want to be noticed by anyone, but even more, I didn't care to be asked questions. There would be questions. Lots of questions. I hoped tea wouldn't last a long time.

Two young maids on the stairs moved to one side until we were past. I meant to smile, but they kept their eyes down and curtsied to Ivy, who paid them no mind at all. There were paintings hung on the wall all the way up the stairway—paintings of men and women and even one of Ivy.

The nursery was jammed with a mishmash of too much stuff—balls, dolls and perambulators, wooden jigsaw puzzles, board games and cards, and a tall blue dollhouse with a front tower and white gingerbread trim just like her house. There was a fake lawn and a black spiked fence that marched around it. It had trees and shrubs and flower gardens. I went right over to it. The house was open in the back and had four stories of rooms, just like the real ones, with furniture and rugs, chandeliers and lamps, a glass room with plants, a grand piano, a harp and a mandolin, fake food on the table, and tiny plates and tea things. There were servants galore, a father with a mustache and mutton sideburns, a stout mother, one boy, and Ivy—all in fancy dress.

"What do you do with it?" I asked, breaking my rule about questions. I wanted to touch the things, move them around. But it didn't seem as if there was much to do except look at it.

"What do you think?" she asked.

"It's some sort of game?"

"No, not a game. It's to play with, though," she said.

"Play what?" I asked.

"Just play," she said. She leaned closer. "Sometimes, I play that I am in charge of the house. Governess can't yell about lessons; Father and Mother can't tell me to go away and leave them alone. My brother can't break things and blame me when he's home on holiday. In the dollhouse, everybody has to be nice to me."

"Oh," I said, feeling a tiny bit sorry for her.

"Would you like to play with it?"

"No, thank you," I said, clasping my hands behind me. But I did awfully want to touch the little tea things with the tiny blue flowers on them that made me think of Ma's fairies. Ma would love the miniature pieces of furniture and the dishes and the piano. She would be good at pretending it was a fairy house. She would tell me what the fairies were wearing and their names and what they talked about and how they sang and danced. I tried pretending for her, but I wasn't any good at seeing things that weren't really there. But Ma said the fairies were real. It was sort of queer when she'd started talking to them, but I played along because it made her happy.

Thankfully, a maid brought in the tea things and set them on a small table, not a dull school table but a deep red one, a copy of the one downstairs, polished so bright I could see my face in it. I placed my crisp white napkin across my lap and was real careful to keep my elbows off the table, but my knees bumped the underside no matter how I bent them. I knew Ma would have been a perfect lady, but even that was a sort of pretend too hard for me.

"Of course," Ivy said, "you know why your mother ran off and won't come back?"

I sucked in my breath. My throat froze up, my heart battling the current like a big ole trout under the river ice. I shook my head, but my words were still froze solid. Didn't they know she had died?

She looked disappointed for a second; then she got the smug and superior look she'd worn yesterday. "No one knows for sure," Ivy said. She looked toward the door. "Mother said I shouldn't . . ." She stopped and broke off a morsel of what looked like a plain old biscuit to me but what Ivy called a scone. She popped it into her mouth.

*Go on. Tell me,* I wanted to yell at her. Instead, I sipped my tea and nibbled around the raisins plump as horseflies.

"You really don't know?" she asked.

"No," I said, and glared at her until she blinked.

"I'm not supposed to tell. . . ." she whispered.

The door opened and the stout, overdressed woman from the dollhouse came in. "How are you getting on with your new little friend, sweetness?" she asked, shaking her curls. She did a lot of gasping for air, and her corset made creaking noises when she moved. And no wonder, it was cinched so tight that she was swollen up like a fat bread loaf on top.

"You promised you'd leave us alone," Ivy said, and then pressed her lips together.

"Mother only came to meet your new friend," she said. "Her mother and I were girls together." She creaked closer and stopped. I got a whiff of something smelly like medicine. She leaned down and studied my face. "Why, you're not a bit like Lily. You are Lily Greymoor's child, aren't you?" she asked, straightening but still staring.

"Yes, ma'am," I said, looking down, humbled by my

sorry looks again. "I'm Hattie Belle, and Lily Greymoor's my mother."

Mrs. Vandermeer stood panting over the table for a minute. "I just can't believe it, after all these years," she said a little too brightly. "We're all curious about things, about your mother. . . . She was always so demure," she said. "How is your mother? Did she come with you?"

I pressed my lips together and shook my head. I wasn't about to tell these nosy folk that my mother had died almost a year ago.

"Mother, please," Ivy said.

"Yes, yes," she said. "When you come down after tea, we'll talk." Still drooling with questions, the fat woman shook her head and wheezed her way back to the door.

As soon as the door closed, Ivy burst out, "Well, I'm not supposed to tell, but I don't have to do what she says." She breathed hard, her nostrils flaring, her voice soft. "It's about your grandfather, really. He disappeared, you know. But everyone thinks—the talk is—that he was offed."

"Offed?" I asked.

"You know . . . done away with."

"Done away with?"

"By your grandmother. Gone in the middle of the night. Planted somewhere on the grounds—that's what everyone said at the time and everyone still believes, according to Father." Ivy sat back, looking quite pleased with herself.

"You think my grandmother—? She's no bigger than a songbird . . ." I squeaked, shaking my head. A sick feeling spread through me, and I felt my face go white. Maybe that was why Rose had blustered about me snooping in the cellar. Maybe the cellar hid more than silver and a broken watch, a watch engraved with *WEG. G* for Greymoor. I gasped and quickly covered my mouth. He was buried down there or maybe sealed up in one of those hollow brick arches.

"Don't you see? It's why your mother ran off with that strange man. . . ."

"My father," I corrected.

"Yes, well . . . she knew. That's why she won't come back, because it's too much for her to bear. I'm right, aren't I?"

It must have shown in my face that I believed her, because Ivy's look turned important and knowing again. Grandmother could be unkind. Was she the very darkest sort of wicked, too? "Why would my grandmother do such a thing?" I asked.

"Millstone around her aristocratic neck. That's what

Father says. He says Mr. Greymoor had wild schemes and no business sense. Nearly ruined the family's name and fortune and had to be gotten out of the way. Your mother never told you, did she?" Ivy said, looking smug.

I shook my head vigorously. Ma had said good things about Grandmother, how she had given her the most watchful care, protected her from things. What things? I wondered uneasily. But Ma had loved the thorny old buzzard too.

"If she poisoned him or something worse," Ivy said, dropping her voice to a mysterious whisper, "he'd be haunting the place. Is it haunted? Steps creaking, curtains moving by themselves, strange noises?"

I started to shake my head, then thought better of it. "Yup," I said, another lie rolling like water off my tongue. "Strange knocking sounds and a chill wind and doors opening," I said, hoping to scare her. The darkness at Grandmother's began to seem quite spooky to me. But Ivy wasn't frightened. She hung on every word like I was waving lollipops in front of her.

"Thank you for tea," I said politely. I stood up and inched toward the door.

"You know what this means, don't you? It's your turn now," she said.

I scowled. "Turn for what?" I asked.

"Now you have to invite me over to tea," she said. "We can have a séance, like Mother does with Madame Blatzinsky. We'll conjure up your grandfather's ghost."

I shook my head. I didn't know what a séance was, but it sounded creepy. And I didn't want Ivy snooping around my grandmother's, trying to bring back my dead kin, no matter how much I wanted to know the truth. "Can't for a while," I said, trying to look sorrowful. "The tutor's come up from New York and I'm badly behind on lessons. Years, maybe," I added.

"You'll ruin everything if you don't," she said in warning. "My mother—"

But I didn't let her finish. "You better not say one word to your mother or I'll have to scalp you," I said. "I'm strong and right handy with an ax."

Ivy gasped and backed away, her eyes getting fearfully wide. "You're just like her, your grandmother," she said.

Seeing my chance, I soared down the stairs and flew down the walk in the driving rain without waiting for the stuffy overdressed servant to walk me. A carriage was stopped in front of the gate, and a mysterious black-veiled woman, be-ringed and rolling in tiers of black lace, was coming up the walk toward me, a servant escorting her under a large umbrella.

Before I could dart around her, she grabbed my arm with a powerful grip and pulled me out of the rain. I caught a whiff of whiskey and smoke and saw ashes scattered in her flounces. "So, they've snared the wild bird, have they?" she said in a deep, raspy voice.

I tried to jerk free, but she was stronger. "It's all right, child. I just wanted a look at you." She turned my hand and studied my palm. "Your life line," she said, running a finger in an arc from the side of my hand to my wrist. "And this line running alongside is an attendant line—a guardian angel who flies along beside you and protects you. You'll need that."

"Who is the guardian angel?" I asked, hoping it was my mother.

"No one knows everything. Not even a clairvoyant and medium," she said, gently closing my fingers over my palm. "Grave troubles lie ahead. Someone from the past will seek you. . . . Frightful, unspeakable things will be revealed." She shook her head sympathetically. "You have a strong heart, a good head, and an angel. Mind your words, little bird. Now fly."

# CHAPTER EIGHT

I fled from the palm-reader, chilled by her warning and by what Ivy had said. I viewed Grandmother's house with a hard eye and saw for the first time how shabby things really were—peeling paint, rug worn down to the thread in places, cloudy prisms and tarnished brass on the smallish chandelier, which I had never seen lit, though the front entry was dark. Mainly, I thought about the empty places on the walls and up the stairway, empty places where paintings of Ma and Grandmother and the rest of the family should be, and I thought about Grandfather, a ghost that nobody wanted to talk about.

Grandmother appeared in the doorway looking anxious, Rose's grim face hovering behind her, meat cleaver in hand. When I saw the glint of the sharpened steel, I thought about Rose whacking off chicken parts and her warnings about my breaking anything.

Shuddering, I knew who the real murderer was. How could anyone have suspected Grandmother with Buzzard Rose in the house? My teeth began to chatter, and I shivered violently.

"We must get you out of those wet things before you catch your death of cold," Grandmother said, rushing forward. "You look as if you've seen a ghost!"

That's how I felt too.

"Bring some towels to the kitchen, Rose," Grandmother said.

"Nothing but trouble, that one," Rose muttered as she stomped off to the linen closet. Grandmother hustled me into the kitchen and up next to the stove and helped me out of my dripping dress. "I must see about getting you more clothes. I should've taken care of that already, but—"

"I know—hard times," I said.

"Is that what Ivy Victoria is saying?" Grandmother asked just as Rose came in with towels.

I nodded solemnly, went over the rules of conversation in my head, and kept still. I was pretty sure Grandmother wouldn't question me in front of Rose, and I was right about that.

Grandmother rubbed me down with the towels. "My poor wet little mouse," she said with a sudden rush of affection. As she continued to rub, she sang:

*"Rain on the green grass,*
*and rain on the tree,*
*and rain on the housetop,*
*But not on me!"*

Grandmother knew that song? Hortensia the Cold? Yet when she sang, it was as though Ma had stepped into the room, tousling my hair, the singsong lilt in her voice, calling me her little mouse.

"Did you sing that to my mother?" I was so wet, it wouldn't show if I had tears in my eyes. "Did you call her your little mouse?"

"Why, yes. It's been years since I even thought of it," she said, squinting. "She sang it to you too, then?" Grandmother said, rubbing thoughtfully now, looking hopeful.

I nodded. "Lots of little tunes and poems for her little mouse," I said slowly.

Grandmother stopped rubbing altogether, and we looked at each other without a sound. For a moment it felt like Ma was there smiling sweetly at us, her golden hair braided and wrapped around her head like a halo, her arms twined through ours, making our circle complete.

Grandmother's mouth twitched. "Let's put you in the library while your dress dries," she said finally, a catch in her voice.

Once in the library, Grandmother gave me a warm throw and fussed about, turning up the gas and tucking another soft shawl over my feet. She hummed softly and then quietly said, *"This is Mab, the mistress fairy, that doth nightly rob the dairy. . . ."* She stopped and looked cautiously at me.

It was Ma's milking and butter-churning song, one of her favorite fairy poems. Quietly, I took up the thread, not wanting to break the spell. *"And can hurt or help the churning (as she please) without discerning,"* I continued, my heart pounding. Had all the happy songs Ma taught me come from Grandmother? But Grandmother wasn't the make-believe sort, so how had Ma's fairies become more than just songs and pretending?

Rose stumped in then, carrying a large brown parcel. "Can't get any work done around here since that one came."

"What's that?" Grandmother asked.

Rose huffed. "It's addressed to the miss from that Vandermeer woman."

Grandmother took the package and handed it over to me.

"Here's scissors for cutting the string," Rose said, pulling a small, pointy pair from her apron pocket and making the blades go *snick-snack* with a very telling sound.

I snipped the string, the brown wrapping opened, and the dresses of Ivy Victoria fell out along with a note:

How grand to meet you, Lily's child, at last. I intended to send this package along with you, but you left quite suddenly. Never mind. We're quite anxious for your invitation to Ivy. Don't be tardy about it. Regards to your grandmother.

*Mrs. Cornelius Blackmore Vandermeer*

Grandmother raised her eyebrows. "Well, Hattie, what do you think of Ivy's castoffs?"

"I'll wait for my own dress, please," I said.

"I'd rather that too," Grandmother said, looking thoughtful.

Rose gathered up the unwanted gowns, then went out with Grandmother close behind.

But Grandmother was soon back, bustling in with a sewing basket in one hand and some other gowns thrown over her arm. She sat on the edge of the chaise next to me. Head bent, she brushed her hands gently over the pinks and lavenders and creams as if petting them. For a long time, she said nothing. Then, "These were your mother's," she said quietly. "I've saved them all this time. I don't know why, really. Everyone gives to charity or to cousins, but I couldn't give these away."

My heart beat savagely. I wanted to ask where she was keeping my mother's things. I wanted to ask to see the violet room, but Grandmother looked too sad to be asked anything. I reached over and stroked the material. I yearned to see the gowns shook out, so I could properly imagine how Ma must have looked in them.

"Of course you're much thinner and the gowns aren't fashionable now, but I might alter them," Grandmother said. "You deserve something of your own, but would you mind made-over gowns?"

"No," I said, swallowing. "I'd love to wear something of Ma's. Would you mind very much, Grandmother?"

"No," she said. "It would please your mother, Hattie. Don't you think?"

I nodded. "I can't stitch nearly as fine as Mother, but I could help," I said, suddenly wanting to do something nice for Grandmother.

She sucked in her breath when I said that, held it like she wanted me to go on and say something more about Ma, about the fairy songs we sang, maybe. But somehow, I thought it better not to tell Grandmother about Ma's fairies becoming real to her. "Can you hear the fairies in the hemlocks?" Ma would say to me. All I heard was the wind. "See their gossamer wings?" All I saw were rainbows on raindrops or crystals of frost. She would tilt her head and smile. "They wish me to sing and dance with them," she would say. "Will you dance too, Hattie Belle?" The fairy make-believe was mostly enchanting. But I didn't want to dance about in the clearing with invisible things or answer them like they were asking me questions or telling me what to do.

"She was good with everything she did with her hands and her heart," I said.

"She was," Grandmother said.

"So good that it was hard to believe she could be real," I said, watching her closely.

Grandmother and I looked at one another, not knowing how to go on. But it was a good beginning for both of us. It felt all over again like Ma's golden light was in the room with us.

Grandmother stood up and smiled. "The help with altering is gratefully accepted," she said warmly, "but what shall we do with Ivy's dresses? I suppose we could make some new napkins for tea."

"I'm not inviting her for tea," I blurted out, though the thought of Ivy using her own dresses for a napkin was tempting. "We don't have to do what they want," I said. "Her mother just wants her to snoop. They're all wondering about Ma."

"It's been a while since anyone has bothered with us. Perhaps it would be best not to take on the old regime again," Grandmother said, picking up a lavender dress. "Let's try these gowns, shall we?"

I nodded and got off the chaise.

"My, you really are just bones," Grandmother said, getting a look at me in just my chemise. "Of course, Lily was always plump. She needed a corset by the time she was fourteen, so we'll see, won't we?"

All I could do was bite my lip and hold my breath. But the gowns fit better than either of us expected. The length was good, and with a few well-placed pins and some basting in the bodice, I was fitted out in Ma's lavender brocade. The gown felt soft on my skin, nearly as soft as Ma's fingers brushing over my cheeks. I bit my lip again, hard, to stop me from getting tearful.

Grandmother sniffled and coughed slightly, holding her handkerchief against her lips. "You do look fine, Hattie Belle," she said, and moved quickly on. "I did think there was something more you wanted to tell me about your tea today."

There was something I thought it safe to ask. "What does *demure* mean?" I asked.

"Did someone say that about Lily?" Grandmother asked.

"Yes," I said slowly. "But what does it mean?"

"Shy . . . often withdrawn," Grandmother said.

"Was my mother like that when she was a girl, too?"

Grandmother nodded. "Not with me . . . or Rose. She was often quietly happy at small parties and croquet on the lawn with a few friends, but oftentimes she would get ill before a larger society party. Sometimes she didn't want to be with anyone but me or Rose. She was just shy, my Lily."

"Like Beth in *Little Women*?"

"Exactly so," Grandmother said. "I'm guessing she didn't change when she went away, when you were growing up, then?"

I shook my head. Somehow it loosened something in me to know that Ma had always drawn away from folk, that it wasn't from living with Pa and me that had made her that way. She'd gotten worse, though, about going where anyone might stare at her—wouldn't go to Pepacton anymore even. Pa had done all the shopping.

Grandmother simply nodded and worried her collar again. "I've got to go out tomorrow. I'll be gone most of the day."

"Where are you going? Can I go?" I asked. The thought of being in the house alone with Buzzard Rose was much too frightful.

Grandmother shook her head. "It's business." She stared off for a moment, looking thoughtful. "It's all right, Hattie." Grandmother patted my hand. "There's time for everything." She took a deep breath and walked over to the window. To my surprise, she pinned back the drapes and let the gray light come in. "Much better, isn't it, even if the light is still poor today?" she asked.

I walked over to stand beside her and stared out on the reds and yellows and purples of the flower garden. "Ma always talked about the flowers," I said.

"She would do that," Grandmother said.

"She loved the flowering plum Pa bought her and the bouquets of violets I picked for her best."

"Yes," Grandmother said. "Lily loved the shades of purple." She sighed. "You'll be spending most of your day tomorrow with the tutor. He's been busy putting together an exam for you, to see where you stand in your schooling. When this dreary weather lets up, I'll give you some lessons in horticulture."

"Horticulture, Grandmother?"

She smiled. "Gardening, dear. I'm afraid I've let things go, but perhaps we'll add something. Vinca, maybe, the lilac blue sort with the evergreen leaves—a pretty plant—to fill in the empty places. It grows well even in poor soil."

I stared out at the rain-soaked flower gardens and worried about digging and about the very gruesome thing Ivy had told me.

# CHAPTER NINE

Grandmother was off early the next morning right after breakfast. It was the first I had known her to leave the house, and it seemed strange to see her putting on a long gray cloak to go out in the dreary fog and rain. "I'll be home late—after dark, Hattie. Tomorrow we'll finish altering the gowns."

"Are you walking?" I asked, hoping to learn something of her secret trip.

"Just to the first trolley stop," she said, pulling on her gloves, which were worn and mended and noticeably less presentable than the servant's from next door.

"Are you going on the *Mary Powell*?" I asked, thinking it must be a long trip.

"No, not a liner, just the ferry across to Rhinecliff. I'll catch a train from there."

"To New York?" I asked, trailing Grandmother woefully to the door.

"Don't worry your head about my affairs, dear little mouse." She smiled. "The tutor has the day planned for you. If there is trouble of any sort while I'm gone, you must speak to Rose. Despite her gruffness, you can trust her." She stopped for a minute and looked at me so fondly that it nearly made the dreary foyer glow.

She turned away and picked a parcel off the hall table and set out. I watched her stride briskly down the walk and felt a sorrowful pang as she disappeared. Grandmother was being very kind to me now, and the house seemed different, lonely and unprotected, without her. And despite her words, I was a little fearful of the house and of Rose and her kitchen full of sharpened and handy weapons.

The tutor's exam seemed much the better choice, but he was clearly in no hurry to begin. He came down in his dressing gown for a breakfast tray and the morning papers and took himself back up the stairs, whistling a mournful tune as he went.

I didn't go near the kitchen. I set about dusting the drawing room and the library and polishing the furniture until it shone like Ivy's table. I looked over my shoulder nervously, jumped at the slightest sound, expecting to see the old buzzard Rose come leering around a corner, cleaver in hand, accusing me of something.

After a bit, when Rose didn't appear, I began to snoop around the top of Grandmother's writing desk, hoping to find some room keys. I tried all the drawers, but everything was locked up tight. Grandmother might be fond of me, and I might feel safe with her, but that didn't mean she trusted me with mysteries and secrets.

Finally, I settled down and curled up on the chaise with *Little Women*. I read and read, not wanting to stop for a second. With all these books, who would ever need a school? There must be more than a proper education on these shelves. But Mr. Bottle popped in to announce he was ready to test me.

"Mademoiselle," he called.

I pretended not to hear.

Mr. Bottle came over to me. "Miss Hattie," he said.

I pretended not to see him, and I didn't look up from my book. But it didn't work. With one quick swoop, he grabbed the book from my hands.

I looked up, scowling. But he was smiling, looking quite friendly and sincere. His clothes were brushed and hardly rumpled, and he'd shaved the scraggly little hairs from his chin. I noticed only because of the bloody nicks. I smiled my palest and poorest.

"I promise to get you back to your reading as soon as soon can be," he said cheerily. "If I weren't the tutor, I'd let you go on reading. Never disturb a reading child, I always say. It's bad for her health and a great many other things as well."

"You won't change your mind?" I asked suspiciously.

"Indeed not, mademoiselle."

I went along up the stairs behind him, wondering what sort of exam he was going to give me, and if it would be very hard and long. I stopped by the closed-off room in the narrow passage. As soon as the tutor disappeared into the schoolroom, I slowly turned the knob on the mystery door and leaned on it. I nearly fell in, but I caught myself because I was holding so tight to the knob. I glanced quickly around. In the gray light coming through wavery windowpanes, I could see enough. Grandmother hadn't lied. There was nothing here. Empty as a gunnysack with a hole in it. Maybe there was nothing in any of the other rooms either. Maybe that was the secret. Maybe hard times had taken most everything. Yet I had on a dress of Ma's that Grandmother had kept for years and years. There might be other things—a few small things, at least—and the violet room. Quietly, I pulled the door shut and hurried into the schoolroom.

Through the open doorway into the sitting room, I could see the tutor's open trunk with clothes tossed about, books and papers piled around in a comfortable sort of busy jumble.

The blackboard was empty and waiting, along with fresh sticks of chalk. Mr. Bottle's desk held only a scattered-looking sheaf of papers. The dull brown desk that was mine had a filled inkwell, a pen with extra nibs, pencils, theme book, and copybook.

Mr. Bottle checked the time on his pocket watch, then snapped the case shut. "Are you ready to begin, mademoiselle?"

I nodded solemnly. I was good and ready. I almost blurted out that I had skipped some grades but decided to keep my mouth shut. After all, I hadn't been to school in six months. I might be a bit rusty with my learning.

"We'll begin with the oral exam."

I knew all the answers, flew them back as fast as he could ask, from William the Conqueror and the Magna

Carta to the Declaration of Independence, each and every president and vice president, the states and the territories. I named the continents, oceans, and countries, American authors and their major works. Next, we moved to the blackboard. I conjugated verbs, diagramed sentences, identified clauses, phrases, conjunctions, prepositions, and punctuation. I added, subtracted, multiplied, divided, did fractions and square roots. Pa would be proud.

"Well done, Hattie," Mr. Bottle said. "Excellent work with the lower-level material," he added. *Lower-level material?* He dropped a new sheaf of papers on my desk. "This next part will comprise a shortened version of the sorts of knowledge you will be required to have for entering the Academy."

I looked down, but the words were spelled funny and didn't make any sense. I didn't want to embarrass him, so I flipped over the pages, hoping he'd recovered from his writing jibberish. Maybe he needed spectacles. Phew! On the reverse side was something I could sort out enough to recognize as Latin. But all I knew in Latin were the proper names of the flowers and trees that Ma had taught me, and they weren't even on the page. I looked at the other pages. Algebra, geometry, biology, chemistry, English literature. The exam turned out to be painful. I drooped over the desk. I couldn't even begin to guess what I didn't know, and it was a lot. I would never know enough to go home. I would never see Jasper or Ma's flowering plum. I could only hope that Pa would let me come home even if I didn't have Ma's education.

Tears stinging my eyes, I lifted my head. I looked at Mr. Bottle, pressed my lips together to keep back the sobs, and shook my head sorrowfully.

"You don't know any of it?" he asked. "Surely, there's something . . ." he said hopefully.

I just kept shaking my head, and Mr. Horace Bottle looked about ready to weep along with me. He sighed. "Nothing like starting off with a clean slate."

"Yours, sir, or mine?" I asked hotly.

He looked at me in surprise. "I didn't mean to imply that you lacked intelligence. I just didn't think that you would be quite so . . ."

"Ignorant? Well, neither did I. I don't plan to be here forever, you know," I said.

He lifted his eyebrows.

"Sir," I said. "My pa said I could come home as soon as I got a good education like my ma wanted."

"And I had planned to return to New York by the end of the year to resume my studies," he said gloomily.

"I'll work real hard. I'm no slacker."

"Well, Hattie, we'll both work together for the common good. We may surprise ourselves and have some jolly good times." But he rubbed his chin doubtfully, and I suspected he thought we could never have a jolly anything. Despite his earlier cheeriness, I had an idea that our days together would stretch out as dull and tedious as the snowbound weeks in wintertime without Ma.

Looking horribly lost and woebegone, Mr. Bottle stared out at the rain beating against the window, but he didn't yet know that I was no quitter. I was like a hawk with my wings set for home and my pa.

# CHAPTER TEN

When Mr. Bottle came down for dinner that evening, he didn't look at me or at Rose. He simply began to load up his plate with dumplings and cabbage and carrots, ham and potatoes, like he was the only one who had to eat. I watched him in shocked surprise. Finally, when he'd scooped up yet another ladleful of stew, his arm poised in midair above the serving dish, Rose growled like a mad dog.

His hand hung there, not willing to give up the nice chunk of ham he'd scooped out of the gravy.

"There's other than yourself that needs to eat," Rose said roughly.

The tutor cleared his throat and looked at our empty plates. "Oh, I see. I thought you'd eaten. I was mistaken, I see," he said with a sniff, as if we were depriving him. He sighed loudly, slowly lowered the tidbit back into the pool of gravy.

I lifted my napkin to my lips and giggled. I didn't know which was funnier, the way he shoveled up food or the circular way he talked, like a dog chasing its tail.

But then he swept up his plate and a glass of milk and went to his room, leaving me alone with Buzzard Rose.

"Seen his type before," Rose said as soon as he left the room. "See how he hogged the food without one thought to anyone. That type only thinks about himself. Narcissistic scoundrel."

I didn't offer to defend him, since I wasn't feeling all that friendly about him myself. Curious, but not friendly.

After that, Rose and I cast each other suspicious looks across the table as we filled our plates.

I decided that I should make a stab at friendliness. "I used to do some cooking," I said.

"Really?" Rose said with a snort. "Like what?"

"Stew, mainly," I said. "Rabbit, venison, squirrel. Made

77

bread and biscuits, flapjacks . . . dumplings, too. Never could make pie crust though. Tough as shoe leather, Pa said. Burned nearly everything." I bit into Rose's light and tasty dumpling. "You cook real good, Rose. That's what Ma said, too."

Rose pulled herself up. "Don't think for one minute that I don't see what you're trying to do by being nice. It's not going to work with me," she said, her flabby neck skin waggling like an old turkey's. "I don't care if you are Lily's child. You don't act like her and you don't look like her and my gut still tells me that you're a breaker." Rose broke off and stabbed the air with her fork. "I have a premonition 'bout that."

"I haven't broken anything," I said, feeling a little uneasy about why she kept saying that. Had I broken the brick in the cellar? But how could I? It would take a lot of work to free one of those bricks. Whoever had hidden the small bundle of cutlery and a watch must have chiseled out the mortar on purpose.

"Yet," Rose said. "But it's coming down the road. We'll see what's what then. There's only so much breaking one person can bear, and you'd better not forget it."

I sighed. Rose was talking in riddles. I didn't get it, and

it made my head hurt. I wanted Grandmother to get back. When I heard a noise out on the avenue, I quickly excused myself and ran to the window. I pulled back the heavy drape in the drawing room and looked out. A carriage had pulled up in front of the house next door, and the large woman in black lace and veils was being helped down.

"Rose," I said, swinging around, bumping into her. We both drew back, hissing at each other like two snarling cats. But Rose pushed in right up next to me, peering over my head out the window.

"It's that Madame Blatzinsky again," Rose said. "Ever since Mrs. Vandermeer's mother died, she's been calling in that spiritualist. Quackery, I say."

"Does she do séances?" I asked.

"What do you know about séances?" Rose asked darkly.

"Nothing. Ivy said something about them."

"Spooky nonsense, that's what. It's all made-up hocus-pocus. Can't nobody convince me that you can call back the dead. It's a horrible thing, making money off other folks' grief."

Rose was right about that. "But what if she really can

communicate with the dead?" I asked. "Would you want to do it?"

Rose was quiet. "If I knew it wasn't a hoax, maybe I would want to know about our Lily," Rose said.

"Me too," I said. For a second split up into thousandths, it seemed like Rose and me were close, loving Ma together. It was so quiet that I could feel Rose's heavy breathing against my head, which made the hairs quiver on the back of my neck.

Thankfully, Rose went back to the table. I did too. It was clear by the scowl wrinkling her face that Rose wasn't about to warm up to the likes of me. I wanted to blurt out to Rose that Ma would tell her she'd better not murder me, that I was all right, that I was no breaker.

I picked at the soggy bits of cabbage, cold now, and I studied the pattern of lacy scallops and tendrils polished on my fork, a fork that exactly matched the blackened ones in the cellar. I swallowed my fear of Rose along with those smelly cabbage leaves. "How did my grandfather die?" I asked, watching her face carefully.

Rose choked, then coughed in a gagging way. A piece of carrot flew out of her mouth into the middle of the table. Her face flushed, and her eyes snapped. But she went right back to eating, her head bowed over her plate. Guilty.

Shivery bumps went up my back and over the top of my scalp, but I didn't stop watching her, didn't dare take my eyes off the Grim Reaper.

# CHAPTER ELEVEN

Rose gave up first. Casting dark looks at me, but not saying a word, she got up and started to clear the dishes. As soon as she disappeared into the kitchen, I scooted off to the library. I sat at Grandmother's writing table and wrote to Jasper. I wished that I could talk to him for real and tell him about the bossy Ivy and her scary gossip, Buzzard Rose and her meat cleaver, the queer bundle in the cellar, the strange Mr. Bottle, and most of all how I had been so heartless to Grandmother that she would surely decide to send me away.

But when I started to write, I kept most of the hard-luck stuff to myself and wrote a letter that was dull as my biscuits when I forgot to put in salt, though I hinted strongly at the worst things in the hopes of making him curious to know more and write back or tell Pa to come and get me out of here.

May 9, 1883

Dear Jasper,

I am trying to make the best of things here because Pa thinks it's best for me to be with Grandmother, and I'm trying to get acquainted with her because it would please Ma and Pa. Grandmother is OK, but we don't always know how to act with each other. It's sort of like putting on new overalls that don't fit right and are scratchy and so stiff that they don't move with you and make even a simple sitting down a chore. At first, she scolded me for my country manners, but now I guess she likes me all right. I suspect she still looks down on Pa, and that makes me mad enough to be mean sometimes.

I sure would like to know if you and your pa are still rafting with my pa and who Pa hired to take my place. Somebody bigger, stronger, better, no doubt. I know that rafting is a rough place for a girl to be, but I miss the river and I'm lonesome for Pa and you and your pa every day.

Most of all I wish you could take me to the fair in Downsville come September, like you promised. I was looking forward to sharing a red candy apple and the roasted peanuts you told me about and watching you try to catch a greased pig. I might like to try that myself. I would be glad just to see you. There are too many troubling things here that I can't figure out.

I know you're real busy, Jasper, but if you wrote me even a few lines and wrote a word or two from Pa, I'd be real happy. There is a letter in here for him that I'm sending along with yours, because I know your family goes to town more often to pick up mail. I sure do miss you, Jasper.

Your best friend,
*Hattie Belle Basket*

I blew on the pages till the ink was dry, folded the letter, and slid it into one of Grandmother's pale gray envelopes. It wasn't the letter I wanted to write, not entirely, but I couldn't tell Jasper about my grandfather being offed. It might not be true, but if it wasn't, what had happened to him, and why did Grandmother and Rose get so rattled every time I asked about him?

Then I took a clean piece of stationery and began a letter to Pa:

May 9, 1883

Dear Pa,

I thought Grandmother would have lots of rules and I thought she'd be stricter than the schoolmarm, and I was right. It's OK because she's kind to me now and I guess she's gotten used to my woodsy ways. I think she would like you real good too if she got to know you the way me and Ma did. There's so much that I don't know about what happened to make Ma run off and never come back. Why did Ma tell me that Kingston was too far away forever and ever? What happened? Do you know anything about my grandfather? Nobody wants to say much about him. If you know, I'd be real grateful if you got Jasper or that lawyer in Downsville to write it down for me.

Here I am chattering on with the pen the same

as I do with my tongue. Guess the cabin is real quiet on these dark, rainy days without me, unless you play the harmonica I gave you. Have you seen any of those dark wood violets Ma loved or the pretty May flowers yet? Guess Ma's plum tree will be in blossom now. I sure am lonesome for you, Pa, and I miss your good teasing and your big laugh. Maybe you'll take me with you on a rafting trip again sometime. I sure would like it if you came to visit me here as soon as you can.

The tutor hopes to be done with me and go home by Christmas. I think that is a good plan for both of us, but I wouldn't mind if it were sooner. What do you think?

Your girl,

*Hattie Belle Basket*


I took some coins Pa gave me from my hiding place, slid the envelope between the pages of *Little Women,* and started up the stairs on tiptoe so that Rose wouldn't hear me and so that I could hear her or any other noise in the house.

I stopped on the second-floor landing and peered up into the inky darkness. Pale light was shining out from beneath the tutor's door onto the floor of the passage-way. Why not go on, I decided, and ask the tutor about posting the letter. When I stepped into the narrow passageway, a cold draft, like icy fingers, rippled across my ankles. Shivers went up my arms, but I went on, and knocked, forgetting that the door didn't latch tight. The door creaked opened. The tutor had tossed a blanket on the floor and was lying belly down with a lamp next to him. He was writing furiously. "Drat that bloody door," he cried. Then he looked up.

I was about to turn and flee, but surprisingly his face brightened when he saw me. "Hattie, have you brought me some cakes?"

I noticed his plate then, pushed toward the door, with not a drip of gravy or a scrap of fat on it. He must have licked it. Even a finger run across wouldn't get a dish that clean.

"Sorry," I said. "No cakes."

"A bit of pudding or custard, a slice of pie?"

I shook my head. "We only get sweets at teatime, mostly. Sundays for dinner and holidays, I suppose."

"Well . . . take my dishes down then," he said. "The cook doesn't like me," he said sorrowfully. "I'd rather not see her just now. She growled at me. You heard her."

"She doesn't like me either," I said. "And I'd rather not see her just now myself."

"How might I get on her good side?" he asked, rising up and leaning on an elbow.

"It's no use trying to find her good side. She doesn't have one. She dislikes everyone except Grandmother." I paused for a second, wavering about whether to ask him to mail my letter. I could never ask a favor of him if I wasn't in the least obliging myself. I sighed. "Might as well take your dishes and rinse them myself." I picked up his plate and silver and stacked them on top of the book with the letter jutting out. I took a deep breath. "If I gave you the coins for stamps, would you post a letter for me in town? Rose sees everything and thinks I'm a sneak. Besides, I don't know where to post a letter," I said, not letting on that I wasn't allowed out on the street alone . . . yet.

"Of course I'll post a letter for you. I've a couple myself," he said.

I breathed a sigh of relief. "Thanks ever so much," I said. I eased the envelope out of the book and set it down with the coins on top.

He grinned pleasantly. "Hmm . . . you're quite a writer yourself, I see."

I shook my head. "More a chipmunk filled with chatter, I'm afraid. That's what my pa always said."

Mr. Bottle studied me with interest. "You're a funny child, Hattie Belle—a little strange but nice," he said. "I quite like your hair. It's extraordinary, thick and wild. Such a rich nutty brown too."

I gave him a quick, scowling look. I couldn't tell if he was making fun or not. "Nobody likes my hair. I don't like my hair. It was an accident, and it makes me look like a boy," I said.

"Accident? What was an accident?" the tutor asked with a very curious look.

"I asked my pa for a new dress, but he bought me overalls instead. He said I looked like a boy, so I might as well dress like one. Then I cut off one of my braids. I was sorry, but there was no help for it. I had to cut off the other one too."

"You thought he wanted you to be a boy?" Mr. Bottle asked.

"What else would I think?" I said hotly.

"A great many things," Mr. Bottle said. "But he probably wanted you to do something that girls aren't supposed to do."

"Like what?" I said.

"Drive a stagecoach, be a train engineer, play football, sing in a boys' choir, be the lead male in an opera or a theater production of Shakespeare, or run for president of the United States."

"That's silly," I said with a grin.

"But rather fun to imagine," he added. "Why did he have you dress like a boy?"

So I told him about Pa taking me to work with him and about the river trip and the rough taverns where we stayed and how important it was that no one knew I was a girl, just as Mr. Bottle had guessed.

"Amazing and wonderful. Not something I would be brave enough to attempt," Mr. Bottle said. "You don't look like a boy, though. You look like a heroine, someone valiant and brave like Joan of Arc."

"And burned at the stake," I muttered, ducking my head, but blushing with happiness at this unexpected kindness.

Mr. Bottle hooted. "Not you. Not without a good fight!"

I nodded, getting a nice warm feeling like when I'd met Jasper. I felt my way down to the landing then, worried that Grandfather's ghost was coming along with me and would brush over me like a cobweb. As I started down the last flight, shivers started up my legs and arms. This time I was going down, down, down to killer Rose, and it was almost too frightful. I longed to hear the front door fly open and Grandmother come rushing in.

When I got to the dining room, Rose had pulled a chair over to the window and was leaning forward, looking out. "Rose," I called softly, thinking it best not to startle her. "I've brought the tutor's dishes down. I'll just rinse them."

"Leave them on the table there," she said, sounding more tired than cross.

"Does Grandmother go away on business very often?" I asked as I set the dishes down very gently to make sure I didn't clatter them or, worse, break the plate.

"Often enough," Rose said. "Oh, I wish she'd waited till the weather cleared. There's still a heavy mist, and the fog is thick as a storm cloud." Rose was rocking back and forth. "I wish she'd hire a hansom cab instead of walking from the trolley. It's dangerous for a lady to be alone on the street at night."

"She'll be back tonight, won't she?" I asked. Forgetting my fear of Rose, I walked over to look out. The mist pressed against the windowpane. The gaslight on the foggy avenue looked to be no more than a lighted match.

"Can't we do something? Couldn't Mr. Bottle go to the station with me and wait for her so she'll be safe?"

Rose sighed. For a short instant, she touched my arm. I nearly screamed but held it back. "She's a strong woman, strong as they come," Rose said. "The last thing she'd want would be for you to be out on a night like this, with or without the tutor. *Hmpf*—you'd be more protection for him."

"Might I wait with you, please?" I said, pressing closer to the window for any sign of Grandmother.

"Trains will be slow going in soupy weather like this," Rose said, but her voice was gentle now. "Best for everyone if you get to bed."

"I'll be quiet as a mouse, Rose. No bother or trouble at all."

For a minute I got a feeling that Rose didn't fancy waiting alone and was weakening. Then she sighed. "Hattie, it's what your grandmother would want," she said in a way that made her seem like a different person, like the patient and understanding Rose that Ma had talked about.

Though Rose had tried to put a comforting skin on Grandmother's lateness, I couldn't help but worry. What if Grandmother never came back? What if something happened to her? I backed away and fled up the stairs to my room. I undressed for bed, lit my lamp, and opened the door so I would know when Grandmother got home. I read for a while, but the fog found its way into my chest, filled my throat, stung my eyes, pressed in on me like the mist against the windowpane.

After a very, very long time, I heard the welcome sound of the front door and the hushed voices and Grandmother coming up the stairs. I quickly closed my eyes and let my book fall from my fingers. I breathed slowly, deeply, like I was asleep. I heard her stop and then come into the room and up to the bed. She brushed my hair back, away from my face, leaned over, and softly—ever so softly—kissed my hair just the way Ma used to, and I was safe again.

She stood there a moment longer, then extinguished the lamp and went out.

I lay in the darkness and loved her so much it hurt my heart and made me want to hate her to save myself. But it was no use. I was mired in deep, and it made everything so very hard. I knew then for sure that I loved her, my grandmother, and there was no help for it.

# CHAPTER TWELVE

The dark, dismal rain was over. Sun dappled through my windows and across my bed, and robins chirruped somewhere close by. I washed and dressed in a hurry and rushed downstairs.

I had overslept, yet Grandmother was only just laying the table for breakfast. The drapes were still pinned back, and morning light streamed into the room. Even though the worn rug, the faded wallpaper, and the furniture looked more shabby in the bright light, the room was much cheerier.

Grandmother looked up and smiled, her tired face melting with warmth when she saw me. I quickly looked away, afraid that she would guess that I loved her and was very glad that she was back. I hurried to the sideboard to be near her and breathe in her comforting lilac smell. "Were you home very late?" I asked nonchalantly, taking the plates from her hands.

"Quite late, yes," she said.

"Rose was worried. She sat by the window and wrung her hands," I said, setting the plates.

Grandmother nodded. "Yes, that's what she said."

Heat rushed up my neck. I suppose Rose had told her that I had wanted to go after her, but had she also told her that I had asked about how Grandfather died? I ran my finger over a chip on the plate. "Did Grandfather break things?" I blurted.

"Sometimes," she said with that sound of alarm in her voice whenever I asked about him. "What a strange question. Whatever made you ask such a thing?"

She was doing it again, asking questions back instead of simply answering mine. "Don't know," I said. But I did know. I was wishing someone would tell me. What happened to my grandfather and what made my mother leave here and never come back? "Would you like me to call Mr. Bottle for breakfast?"

"Oh my, no," she said. "He was up before any of us were stirring. He's out in the kitchen helping Rose. Apparently the sunshine agrees with him."

"In the kitchen with Rose?" I squeaked. "Up early?" He was trying to get on Buzzard Rose's good side. Well, he'd see it was not so easy.

But maybe if you knew how to flatter her the right way, you could find a side to her that wasn't like a briar patch, because, wouldn't you know it, Mr. Horace Bottle came sashaying out of the kitchen with a platter stacked with pancakes and a pot of coffee. He was whistling like a songbird, his cheeks a healthy pink, and he had one of Rose's aprons wrapped around him. "Good morning, madame. Good to have you back. Good morning, mademoiselle." He placed the platter on the table near his place setting, and as he leaned down, he gave me a broad wink.

Alarmed, I wondered if he was winking because he'd found Rose's good side or did the wink mean that he knew my letter was a secret between us?

Rose bustled out, carrying a plate of sausages and a pitcher of syrup. She patted her hair and smoothed her dress before sitting down. She wasn't smiling, exactly, but there was a certain noticeable lack of scowls. What could he have possibly said or done to make Rose change so quickly? Last night she had growled at him like a dog.

I took a couple of pancakes but passed on the fat sausages that reminded me of Ivy's curls. Mostly, I picked at my breakfast. The important thing about picking at food, taking small bites with long in-between spaces for chewing, was to keep from missing anything at the table. Pa said hawks were alert and watchful. Take a bite, glance around for danger, take a bite. At the moment, I was watching as the tutor piled pancakes and sausages on his plate and spilled a river of syrup over them. He was enormously entertaining when he ate. He sniffed his food and slurped a bit and sometimes forgot to close his mouth when he was chewing.

"It was very generous of you to go out to the butcher's shop this morning and bring back this lovely sausage," Grandmother said. "But you really musn't make a habit of it."

"Why not?" Rose said a bit crossly. "He's like a starved

animal. Why shouldn't he help with putting food on the table?"

"No, Madame Greymoor, I assure you"—Mr. Bottle's healthy pink turned bright red—"I just favored a fat, juicy sausage this morning."

"I favor sausages myself," Rose said, giving the tutor a very fond sort of look that meant her good side was found after all, but Horace was too busy cutting up his sausage to notice how she beamed at him.

Maybe he hadn't mailed my letter after all. He'd been out, but maybe he just used my coins for food, and there was nothing I could say or do about it here at the table. I would have to wait.

The tutor recovered his humor soon enough. "How was your trip yesterday, ma'am? Business good?" he asked.

Grandmother and Rose exchanged looks, a sort of silent message going between them. Grandmother looked pale and thoughtful. I didn't think she was going to answer him at all. "About the same," she said quietly. "No noticeable improvement. Next trip, perhaps."

The tutor sighed deeply, thinking about the hard times here, no doubt, and his stomach, in particular, and there was no more talk at the table after that.

It worried me too, being a burden and a bother, and I didn't take seconds so that Mr. Horace Bottle wouldn't look so wounded and deprived.

Later, in the schoolroom, Mr. Bottle confessed. "I did post the letters, honestly. I'm not completely dishonest, and I only pinched what was left over. But who could blame me when I walked by the shop and they were hanging up those fresh, meaty sausages. I could nearly hear them sizzling in the pan, and the aroma. Drat it all. I thought I had the old...old..."

"Buzzard, sir?"

"Yes, apt description," he said, and went on. "Flummoxed. She's gone from growling to barking. I suppose she bites too," he ranted.

"There's a good chance of that," I said, thinking of Grandfather and of my far-fetched suspicions about Rose, but somewhat cheered that the tutor and I were in agreement about her.

"Ah, I bet she pecks at the eyes and claws out hearts." He stopped and looked at me. "Are you put off about the coins, then?"

"Nope," I said with a great shake of my head. It was quite a relief to me that he wasn't a blackmailer like Ivy, which would have put him on the list of good reasons *not* to be in Kingston.

Actually, for the first time it seemed as if the wind had finally shifted in my favor, getting me back on course. I wasn't counting on it too much, but I did feel a glimmer of hope. At least I knew Mr. Horace Bottle was my friend, and that was something.

# CHAPTER THIRTEEN

I spent the summer waiting for a letter from Pa or Jasper and worrying that I had been forgotten or worrying about what would be in the letter if one did come. I always worried about that but began to worry less about the strange little bundle in the cellar, lost clock keys, and the ghost of my grandfather. I forgot that I wasn't going to like it here. I even forgot all about my short list of reasons to stay in Kingston. Toward summer's end, that's how it felt to me—a contented sort of feeling played across my skin like a lazy breeze, the sort a hawk could drift along on for miles, in peace. But I never forgot about home or Pa and Jasper. Often, I went to the far corner of Grandmother's property, where the tangle of lilac bushes and forsythia protected me from spying eyes. From there I could gaze at the rugged hills and search the trail that Pa might travel on when he came to visit me.

A lot of other good things happened that summer, too, like Ivy Victoria and the lot of them, except her father, going off to summer on Cape Cod, by the ocean. I was digging in the soil and picking rocks out of the vegetable garden with Grandmother the day they left. Ivy called me over to the fence when the last of the trunks were being carried out to tell me about her lovely holiday and to let me know that she was having a grand birthday party when she returned. "You should have invited me for tea," she said, "but since you didn't, we can't be friendly and Mother is crossing you off the invitation list."

"Too bad you're leaving just now," I said, and then I lied: "I'm nearly caught up on lessons and I was going to invite you over for a séance a week Monday when my best friend comes for a visit."

Ivy's mouth dropped open, and she glared at me with her piggy little eyes. "Liar. You don't have a best friend.

Nobody will invite you to any teas or parties or séances with Madame Blatzinsky . . . you . . . scalper."

I reached through the fence and tugged on one of her fat sausage curls.

Ivy gasped and backed away. She ran to her mother, who was standing on the walk, pressing a hankie to her nose and yelling orders shrilly to the bustling servants pouring in and out of the house like alarmed ants. Ivy gave a fearful backward glance over her shoulder. Her mother snatched her arm and went off down the walk toward the waiting carriage. I felt a twinge of something sweet as they drove off. No more Ivy or her horrid mother till the end of summer—no more worries over séances and teas. I smiled.

Another good thing that summer was the tutor, who turned out to be enthusiastic about a great many things. Poetry was Mr. Bottle's passion, and he talked at length about a modern poet, Oscar Wilde. The tutor had heard him lecture on "Art for Art's Sake" in New York the year before. And he confided that whenever he crossed the East River on the Brooklyn ferry, he felt deep kinship to his most beloved bard, Walt Whitman.

The tutor spent a good share of his wages on food for

the table and begged Rose for lessons in cookery and coaxed her to try some of the exotic fare in *Miss Leslie's Cookery Book,* which she did—delightful things, really, like Nasturian sauce or Charlotte Polonaise, and all sorts of delicious fruity cordials for sampling in the evening. And Rose seemed to forget her premonition that I was a breaker, didn't brandish her meat cleaver, and stayed agreeably intent on concocting things not always boiled or fried. She even got a sweetly crooked sort of smile on occasion, most often after a few samplings of cordials, and she quite doted on Horace and beamed whenever he was about.

Mr. Bottle had taken to wearing colorfully patterned vests and had made considerable attempts to grow a mustache or sideburns or a beard, but always failed. He began to take me on Social Studies trips, as he called them, into the town to observe the populace, who, for Horace, always resembled food in some way. It started when he began to compare the ladies in their walking suits and parasols to the French pastries or Italian ices we always indulged in on these trips. Pastries were for the well-endowed matrons, ices for the young and lovely. Working men were meaty roasts of beef or mutton. Businessmen were stuffed partridges, pheasants, and sometimes turkeys if they were portly and seemed very wealthy.

The trolley cars were particularly interesting for Social Studies, he said. The mix of people—the washed and unwashed, the prim with the noisy drunks, the polite with the shocking cursers—all jumbled close together, were often fruits or vegetables—fresh or raw, hot or cold, stewed, colorless, undercooked. . . . It was thoroughly educational, clues to the social classes, Mr. Bottle said, but I enjoyed the entertainment of it more than anything, the specialness of having our own private way of seeing. "There," he would say, winking and pointing his walking stick, "is a prime example of a meaty roast that's overdone and tough to chew."

I didn't even care that I wasn't getting any geometry or chemistry or much geography for that matter. There was time for everything, the tutor said, echoing Grandmother, and he didn't see the point of spending the whole of our summer with Homer or Pythagoras. And chemistry, ideally, would be saved for dead last. I suspected that he was getting quite fond of Kingston and wished to stretch things out.

But I also discovered at the end of the summer that just because you forget about some things doesn't mean that they aren't right next to you all the time, like your shadow, waiting for a certain light to make them grow long and frightful again. That's the way it was. It all changed in a single day.

All of that August had been hotter than the hot place, and the leaves on the fruit trees and the flowering shrubs wilted down, and the grass, burnt brown, crackled under our feet. The flowers and vegetable plants, though drooping some in the day, stayed fresh from our constant watering. The least walking about caused a great deal of sweating, so we did all the necessary chores of emptying the smelly pots and tidying the rooms before the sun was high. The rest of the day we read.

The tutor moved down to the second floor, and lessons moved down to the library. Evenings, when a cooling breeze came off the river, we unlatched the windows and aired the house. In the daytime, the drapes were dropped and the house was dark as the day I'd come.

That last good morning near the end of August, Grandmother had sent the tutor into town for a six-cent loaf of bread for sandwiches and me to the garden with a basket to pull some radishes and lettuces and to pick cucumbers for our luncheon. I gathered some dark green cucumbers and selected the lettuces that had gone reddish at the top but didn't have blighty spots. The radishes were getting woody, so it took longer to find good ones, but where one had gotten fat, another growing next to it had stayed small and tender. I was starting to sweat and the lettuces were starting to wilt, so I yanked out a whole handful of the radishes and a great clod of dirt came along on the roots.

*Thunk!* Something—an old radish, coming loose from the bunch probably—dropped on my toe. But it wasn't a radish and it wasn't a rock. My heart began to beat wildly as I bent down and broke apart the oddly shaped clump. A bent horseshoe nail, maybe. But it wasn't that. I sucked in my breath and stared in horror at the whiteness of the small thing left in my palm. A bone.

I poked the hole where the radishes had been and found another small piece of bone. I dug a little more and unearthed a small key, then a larger one encrusted with dirt and wrapped up in rotted cloth, a swatch of linen like the one wrapped around the silver and watch that I had found in the cellar. How had we not discovered the missing clock keys before when we were planting? Who had done this? What should I do?

The black nasty feeling crawling along the bottom of my stomach came surging up into my throat like a giant wave. Was Ivy right? Was it true then that Grandfather was buried here, in pieces, maybe cut up by Rose's cleaver like the chickens she whacked apart? Had Grandmother helped? Was it possible that my mother had known?

"Hattie!" Grandmother called from the pantryway. "Are you all right?"

"Coming," I called. I kept the keys but dropped the pieces of bone back into the hole and started to cover them over with dirt. But it wouldn't do, would it? I mean, Grandmother would want to know where I'd discovered the keys, and there would be a furious digging in the garden, and maybe there'd be more bones unearthed or maybe nothing. But with my hard luck, it was more likely that they'd sprout up like seedlings.

I didn't know how the keys had gotten there, but I knew that Grandmother would be glad to have them. She said herself that she had looked everywhere for them. Rose was surely the guilty one, though why would she bury Great-Grandfather's clock keys? And even more puzzling, why would she hide the silver? None of it made sense, but it was chilling . . . to the bone. Horrified, I shivered.

"Hattie," Grandmother called again. "Whatever are you holding?"

For a second I couldn't think. How could I get rid of the bones with her watching me? My heart thudding, I called back to her, "Grandmother, I've found your keys." Quickly, I stooped to pick up my basket of radishes and lettuce and dropped the bones in my pocket. Then I hurried to the house. When I reached her, I opened my hand. "Clock keys," I said, giving them to her. "Stuck to the radish roots."

"Clock keys," she echoed. "In the garden. Buried there," she said, looking quite stunned. "I never would've have thought. They must have just now worked to the surface. After all these years . . . I thought they were lost forever. How wonderful that you've found them," she said.

The finding of keys did not seem to bode well with Rose. She gave me a dark, hooded look, the first in several months, which made me suspect her all the more.

"Do you suppose . . . I hate to think . . . couldn't be—" Grandmother started, her face getting pale as the radish centers she would soon be slicing. She broke off, exchanging looks with Rose.

"It was probably that upstairs maid, the upstart, light-fingered one. She knew she was going to be let go. It'd be just like her, Hortensia," Rose said soothingly.

"One of the maids stole things?" I asked, but was

ignored. It must have been the maid who had hidden the silver and not gotten a chance to cart it off.

The color returned to Grandmother's face. "Yes, you might be right. She was here when things disappeared." But I could tell by Grandmother's face that she didn't think it was the maid at all.

Grandmother prattled on: "We'll clean these up and get the clocks going again today. It will be a *very good* thing to hear the clocks again, Rose, a very good thing to get back things that were lost."

"Some things that are lost are better off staying lost," Rose said. Was Rose talking about me? Or had she guessed that I had found more than keys?

But I was stuck with the bones jiggling together in my pocket. Since I was a picky eater, no one seemed to notice that I had less appetite than usual, and, of course, the tutor was always willing to finish up for me. How could I eat a radish that had been in the ground with Grandfather's bones bound around its roots? Or anything grown in the garden for that matter. It was quite horrifying to watch the rest of them crunching away.

But that was only the beginning.

# CHAPTER FOURTEEN

I didn't like to think of Grandfather's bones being in the house—it would make things too creepy at night—but I couldn't throw them away or bury them just anywhere, or we'd dig them up again.

It was hard to do anything without everyone in the house knowing, but I managed to get a small, wooden cheese box from the stack Rose saved in the pantry, line it nicely with some scraps from Ivy's green gown, and gently place the bones in it, still wrapped up in a hankie.

Late that night, while the others were sleeping, I snuck out of my room. Holding on to the banister with one hand and gingerly grasping the tiny coffin in the other, I felt my way down the long, dark staircase. If anything could conjure up my grandfather's ghost, digging up his bones and traipsing around with them in the dark should do it. Just the thought made the hairs prickle on my arms.

When I reached the bottom of the stairs, I stopped and took a deep breath before going on, tiptoeing along the gloomy hallway. The black humped shape of chairs and the pot of ferns with their hairlike fronds seemed to shift restlessly in the darkness of the dining room. I wanted to run past, but Rose slept nearby in a room off the kitchen. My heart beat faster now, but I crept along more slowly. In the dead quiet, I could hear Rose's rasping wheeze broken by an oinking snore that nearly made me drop the box of bones. I clapped a hand over my mouth to squelch a nervous giggle.

Finally, I was out in the warm night brightened only slightly by the gas lamps on the avenue. Cool tendrils of fog wisped around me like ghostly fingers. Crickets chanting in the grass grew silent at my approach. I hurried now, easily following the brick path around to the corner of the house. With my hands, I dug a hole in the loose dry dirt beneath the roots of the rambling rose.

When I had carefully smoothed the dirt over again, I

bowed my head. I knew I should say something good and holy, but I didn't want to use the same prayers and psalms that Pa and me had used for my ma. "Holy, holy," I said. Holy what—cow? I cleared my throat and started over. "I'm pretty sure God doesn't like dead folk to go around haunting the living, so I hope He will take you up to heaven or someplace not too far from it. May God keep you from the hot place and may you rest in peace, Grandfather, and never get the urge to come back here. Amen." I'd look up a little psalm to say another time so if he hadn't gotten to be an angel he might still feel kindly toward me.

Quiet as the fog, I slipped back inside, real glad to be rid of the bones from Grandfather's skeleton, real glad to be safe in my bed again.

It was probably the secret burial in the dark that got me feeling sad and missing Pa more than usual. If only I could hear him play his harmonica or watch him whittling, or if only the two of us could be tipping our chairs back against the cabin and looking up at the starry sky, Pa telling me what all the different sounds were in the forest at night—tree frogs, owls, insects, raccoons. Pa knew the sounds of all the wild things. More than ever, I longed to go home.

The next day, I decided to write another letter so he'd know how powerful lonesome I was for home, but Rose shot me a suspicious look when I came into the library carrying my book. I felt like a sneak. No doubt I looked guilty too.

"There you are," Grandmother said, brightening. "I was beginning to worry. You looked so pale at lunch, hardly touched a bite of food."

"The heat's wearing us all down," Horace said, looking up from his book. He was reading his way through all the really old plays by Marlowe and Shakespeare again. "Her brown skin is fading to white is all, with us closed up in the house every day like I was when I had the fever," Horace said.

The tutor had taken on some rosy color since he'd come, but I didn't like to think that I had his old white-paint pallor. "Am I really pale?" I asked, feeling dismayed. "Not chalkish like Ivy's mother?"

"Yes," said Rose, who was stitching flowers on the new minty green pillow covers she and Grandmother had made from one of Ivy's castoff gowns.

"No," said Grandmother. "Just slightly peaked, that's all. Your color will come back by sundown." Grandmother was always reassuring that way, and I went to sit by her on the chaise. I wanted to, somehow, more than before. Suddenly, I wanted to tell my grandmother about how much it ached inside that I didn't have Ma to go home to. But I didn't want to say it in front of Rose or even Mr. Bottle, who was very kind about things, and my throat hurt from the not telling. Instead, I put my head down in her lap just like I would have with Ma and closed my eyes. "I do feel poorly," I said, but what I really meant was homesick.

No one said a word, but Grandmother brushed her hand over my forehead, brushed my hair off my cheeks, with gentle strokes just like Ma. I breathed in her lilac scent and went to sleep.

I woke up a short time later from the sound of Rose and the tutor bringing in the lemonade and honey ginger cakes for teatime, but no one made mention that I had napped. On the tray was a pinkish envelope with a suspiciously familiar look and smell to it.

It was addressed to me and was, in fact, an invitation to Ivy's party in a fortnight. "Ivy told me I wasn't to be invited," I said.

"Invited to what?" Rose asked, being the least polite of the three.

I wet my lips and wordlessly handed the invitation to

115

Grandmother. I was no longer hungry. "I don't want to go," I said. "When I went to tea, Ivy was only interested in telling me about your hard times. She said that Grandfather lost your fortune and your good name, nearly. She said that he was a millstone. . . ." I nearly blurted out the rest, but I didn't want to hurt Grandmother. I suspected she didn't know the gossip about offing Grandfather and burying him on the grounds somewhere.

"You have to go to the party," the tutor said solemnly. "We'll show them."

"How?" The three of us said at once.

The tutor shook his head and shrugged. "I'll have to give it some thought," he said.

It wasn't a very cheery prospect for me. The tutor was like a large fluttery butterfly, flitting from flower to flower. The party was the most colorful blossom at the moment, but that could be discarded like so many other of his projects with spectacular ease in a moment's time. Rose would be disagreeable if it meant more work for her.

"It will be dreadful. Everyone wants to see Lily's child," I said, "and everyone will ask questions about her and about all of you."

"It would be hard for you," Grandmother said. "It really would be too much to face them all at once."

"But I could do it," I said. "I'm not a chicken, you know."

"Then do it," Rose said. "They're no match for the likes of you."

It was a compliment of sorts, with even a bit of fierce pride and near affection in her voice, which took me aback. "All right," I said. "I'll go."

# CHAPTER FIFTEEN

That evening the clockworks were oiled, the keys for winding satisfactorily cleaned, and two of the clocks wound. They made a very pleasant ticking sound like strong and gentle heartbeats in the library.

"Did you know," I told Grandmother when we were alone that evening, sitting on the chaise together listening to the clocks, "that they don't know that my mother died?"

"You didn't tell them, then?" Grandmother said, sounding relieved.

"No," I said. "Can't seem to talk about it."

"No," she agreed. "It's not an easy thing to do."

"It makes it all come fresh again."

"Yes."

"Is it like that for you, Grandmother?"

For a minute, she kept her head turned away. "Yes, for me, too, Hattie," she said finally.

"There's time for everything," I said, trying to be helpful and comforting the way she was to me.

"Or none at all," she said sadly. "We never really know which, do we?"

"No," I softly agreed. It never seemed the best right time, but this was as close as any, here and now. "Mother told me about her violet room. May I see it, Grandmother? I'd like awfully to see it . . . if . . . Is there anything to see?" I said, faltering.

Grandmother reached over and took one of my hands. "Of course you would want to see it. I thought to open it for you, for you to have as your room, but . . . it'd been so long."

"Is it too hard for you, Grandmother?"

Grandmother shook herself. "Difficult but not impossible. It's time," she said. "I'll get the key."

When we started down the long dark hallway, I had a

keen feeling that Ma's room would be at the very end of the corridor next to Grandmother's room, and it was. I was shaking with a feeling close to the one I had when Pa and me had buried her under the plum tree. Guess this was a grave of sorts, too.

Grandmother looked down at the key, pushed it into the lock, and turned it until there was a click. "There," she said, taking a step back. "Would you like to open the door?"

I took a deep breath and gave the knob a gentle turn. The door swung open as if it were inviting us to come in. And so I did. Ma had always called it the violet room, and I'd always imagined the wallpaper would be like the fabric of a brocade dress, but it wasn't. Thousands of violets—deep purple—were hand-painted on a background of a soft lilac color. There were cobwebs and dust coating everything, and the white eyelet coverlet on the bed was yellowed, and the musty odor tickled my nose. It wasn't until I moved deeper inside that I saw the statue of a marble angel on a bureau, and some angels, like guardians, carved into the window trim at the corners, and the dollhouse—a house built like this one with all the rooms the same.

"There are no people in the dollhouse," I said to Grandmother.

"No, she wanted one without dolls," Grandmother said, walking over to stand by me. "But it was her favorite thing, her fairy house. She wanted it always here in her room—not in the nursery or put away when she became a young lady. Why, look, there are little dresses and cloaks," she said, bending down to peer inside.

A sick feeling came over me like we were caught in a blinding snow together, and I shivered. "She sewed little dresses and bonnets for my clothespin dolls," I said. "She just liked to do it, sew dainty things." I reassured myself that Ma's fairy world had been make-believe and enchanting for both of us until just a few months before she died.

"Yes," Grandmother said slowly, thoughtfully, as if she'd stumbled onto something a bit troubling and sad. I was sad, too. Guess I thought the violet room would make Ma seem alive somehow. But it didn't. They were just things that she'd left behind years before, like wilted flowers with the life gone out of them, empty and lonesome-looking without Ma to make them real.

"Hattie," Grandmother said finally. "Did she . . . ever do anything that wasn't, well, quite like other people?"

I was pretty sure Grandmother was wondering about the little clothes in the dollhouse, but I thought it best not to tell her how Ma had started talking to the fairies. Instead, I shook my head and said, "She was sort of shy about going places, and she seemed to be stuck somewhere in her mind between here and our hills, like she was awful homesick."

"Oh, Hattie . . . she was all right about other things, though?"

I thought about the bugs that weren't real and the time she thought spiders were crawling on her. I swallowed. It had seemed easy enough for Pa and me to explain these things when they happened—a breeze that made the flour dust fly, an itchy rash. But no matter what we said, Ma couldn't be comforted. As if she knew something we didn't. She was horribly melancholy after that; then she got sick with the pleurisy.

"She was sweet as maple sugar and always good and kind," I said fiercely, tears stinging my eyes. "She was like an angel to Pa and me and she was awfully homesick for you, Grandmother."

"Thank you," Grandmother said with a shuddery sigh. "It gives me some peace to know."

I took Grandmother's hand to comfort her. Then we went out and closed the door, but this time Grandmother did not lock it.

* * *

At supper a couple of nights later, Rose remarked that it was odd for the Vandermeers to return before summer's end. Pity they hadn't stayed away—and their invitations too, I sputtered darkly. Everyone solemnly agreed except for the tutor, who delighted in keeping us informed of the constant flurry of deliveries and the return of Madame Blatzinsky.

Three days before the party, my gown was ready for a final fitting. It was altered from one of Ma's, a rich creamy color. The tutor had designed it with bows and ruffles and lace and flounces and tiers, but it didn't turn me into the girlish beauty Horace said I would be; something was wrong. I could see the disappointment in all their faces.

Grandmother came to my rescue. "No offense, Horace. You've created a lovely design to rival any of the girls', but it's all wrong for our Hattie. The whole affair is much too busy."

The three of them stood back and surveyed me with critical eyes.

"It's her short wild hair that makes the dress look all wrong," Rose said.

"I love her hair," Horace said. "It makes such a social statement."

"We could shape her hair, trim the bangs, put a little wave to the sides and the ends," Grandmother said. "Maybe a satin ribbon tied in."

Instead of fluttering away and moving on to a new project, a feverish look came into the tutor's eyes, and his cheeks glowed. He grabbed up his drawing pad and charcoal and started off for the drawing room, where the light was best. "I think I've got it. You'll be the envy of them all, Hattie."

I stared at Grandmother and back to Horace. I didn't want to be the envy of them all, or the talk of the town. I didn't even want to go, exactly. There were too many things to worry about here. No wonder Ma had made up a world of pretends. But off I went with Horace.

Only minutes later, it seemed, Grandmother came flying in, her lips all quivery. "Hattie, Mr. Bottle," she said. "We've a visitor."

"Pa?" I asked. He would rattle her for sure, coming so unexpected-like.

"No, no, it's business," she said. "With my cousin. Could you go into the library? Oh, dear," she said, worrying the lace at her neck, something I hadn't seen her do since I'd first come. "Oh, do hurry, please. I'll bring him around to meet you afterward."

Wordlessly, we gathered up the drawing things and scuttled off to the library down the hall. What sort of business did she mean? I wondered. What dreadful sort was he to put Grandmother in such a state?

Horace bent his head to his work. I listened to the soft swishing of charcoal on paper as the long minutes plodded by. Grandmother finally returned.

As it turned out, Ernest Holmes might have been the bearer of bad news, but he did not seem a bad sort at all. He was short like Grandmother and had kind gray eyes and bushy mutton-chop sideburns gone quite white, and he was neatly dressed in a checkered suit. He spoke politely to the tutor, but he seemed delighted to meet me and took one of my hands and clasped it warmly between his chubby ones. "You're Lily through the eyes," he said, which made me like him altogether. "And you've Uncle Nathaniel's nose."

"Your great-grandfather," Grandmother explained to me. "She does, doesn't she, Ernest," she said, and looked at me proudly, as if I had done something terribly right.

"The clocks are running. You've found the keys, then?" Cousin Ernest said, smiling. "Good fortune for you, Hortensia."

"Hattie found them," Grandmother said quickly, in an even voice. It seemed clear that she didn't care to say where I'd found them.

"Young ones do have the keenest eyes. They see things the rest of us miss," he said, sounding satisfied.

"Exactly so," Grandmother said with a sigh.

When he was leaving, Grandmother put a hand on his arm and walked out with him, their voices trailing into the library as they tarried in the hallway.

"We'll weather this; don't you worry, dear Hortensia," he said in a calming way. "The Cornells don't own the river, but I do think it best to inquire into telephone and electricity and other stock that could be more promising for future financial growth."

"Oh, Ernest, I'm sorry that you've the burden of all this. It does get difficult at our age to hold our own and spring back."

"You've been through worse. How glad I am that Lily's child has come. She must be a great comfort."

"She's brought me joy, Ernest," Grandmother said, and then it was quiet.

I stepped back from the library door, wishing I hadn't heard these last words. It was my own fault for eavesdropping, and now I had sorrowful pangs. It was hard to love two people like I did Pa and Grandmother and not be able to live with both of them, because the truth was, Grandmother's felt like home now just as much as our cabin. I didn't rightly know how to fix that. Maybe there was no fix to it.

Then Cousin Ernest was gone, and Mr. Bottle was impatient to get back to his creation. "I've just put the finishing touches on the new design," he told us when we were all together in the library again. "Notice the simple but striking lines. No bows, no flounces—one tier, a simple eyelet collar and cuffs, ribbon tied at the waist and buttons," he said as he showed us the sketches.

"It's grand, Horace," I said, cheerfully enough, but, truthfully, I thought it horribly plain. I'd look like a stalky, petalless thing sticking up in a garden of girls who were like plump, perfect peonies.

"And an easy makeover," Horace continued.

Rose wore her usual gloomy air. "I'm sorry I ever said she should go, Hortensia. It's not as if I've nothing else to attend to," she said. But, as always, she stayed to help.

Whatever Cousin Ernest had said to Grandmother

during their private conversation, she said nothing of it to me. Not that evening when we were alone in the garden, not at breakfast the next morning, not during our hours of sewing. Nothing was said about Cousin Ernest's bad news. I was haunted by the worried crinkles at the corners of Grandmother's mouth and eyes, but whatever they meant, she was keeping it to herself.

# CHAPTER SIXTEEN

The gown was finally done and fitted just a day before the party. It was plain with all the poof taken out, and I *was* a stalky, petalless thing, except for the deep purple ribbon grandmother had gotten to tie at my waist.

"Striking," said the tutor.

"Why wouldn't she be?" said Rose, with little enthusiasm. "We've done nothing but sew till I'm blind nearly."

"You look like a young lady in blossom," Grandmother said. "Like your mother," she added tenderly.

"Do I, Grandmother, really?" I asked as warmth spread across my cheeks, because I could see in her face that I did, at least to her. She was the only one looking at me and not just the dress, and I met her gaze in a secret sharing of my mother.

While Horace and Rose admired my dress, the sky took on an eerie yellow cast. Black clouds began to race up the river valley, and a cooling wind swept through and stirred the stale air excitedly. Happily, we stepped out the back and stood in the enchanting wind until after the first great splotches of rain sizzled on the dry ground and the rain came drumming down.

It was still raining the next morning, a slow, steady drizzle that promised to last all day.

At breakfast, Rose reported with noticeable glee that the pony rides would be off and lawn games as well, and the tent had been ripped and toppled to the ground. The whole affair would have to be held indoors. "Serves 'em right," she said, and chuckled. It was the first I had ever seen Rose tickled by anything, but that only made everything more dreadful for me, didn't it? The whole lot of us would be packed into the house like sticks in a bundle.

Later in the kitchen, when Grandmother was putting a

wave in the hair that framed my face, I said, "I love the purple ribbon—it was Ma's favorite. Is that why you chose it?"

She nodded. "If only she could see you." For a minute, the only sound was the soft breath of our wishing for Ma to be with us.

I leaned my head against Grandmother for a second. She circled both arms around me and pressed her cheek against my hair. It was comforting to be close to her.

"You don't have to go the party," she said. "But I do believe it's best to face our adversaries, and I've asked Horace to escort you. He's been so devoted to getting you ready and in such a twitter about it."

"Horace will be wonderful at Ivy's horrid games," I said, feeling suddenly happier about the party.

At that moment, Mr. Horace Bottle himself came in all flushed, wearing a new creamy vest that matched my dress. Rose followed close behind. "The carriages have been arriving for a while now," Horace said. "I think we'd better hurry."

Before any of us could add to that, Horace said, "How do I look?"

"Well fed," Rose said.

"Healthy," Grandmother said.

"Like a poet," I added, though I had no idea what a poet was supposed to look like.

"Oh, Hattie, you are always so kind to me," he said, full of emotion, and I was glad I had said it and pleased that anyone should call me kind. Maybe I did have some of my mother's goodness in me after all. "Shall we?" he asked, crooking his arm for me.

I took his arm and we set off with our old umbrella, Grandmother and Rose watching worriedly from the window. As we walked toward the Vandermeers', the carriage of Madame Blatzinsky clattered up the avenue and pulled into the drive, and her warning to me about "grave troubles" came flooding back. I felt that something horrid was about to take place.

# CHAPTER SEVENTEEN

When Horace and I were announced, the girls stopped what they were doing and looked at us—at me—in utter astonishment. Horace patted my hand and leaned down. "French pastries, the lot of them," he whispered.

My heart fluttered, but I smiled bravely around at everyone and searched for Ivy, but I couldn't quite pick her out of the cloud of girls in their pink, poofy gowns, and she didn't come up to greet me. Going over Skinner's Falls with Pa on a raft in the Delaware had been easier than this. At least then I had known what to do with my hands.

Horace nudged me and nodded toward the table, which was decorated with miniature fruits designed to look like colorful shrubbery and plates of confections; an enormously tiered cake, frosted pink, was in the center of the table beneath the glimmering light of the chandelier. Horace was nearly drooling, and I knew he'd be hovering over the sweets as soon as manners allowed.

Mrs. Vandermeer, overly painted and stuffed into her gown, came up to us. "It's like seeing a vision of the past," she said, looking quite unnerved. "You really are Lily's daughter. It must be the dress that's changed you. And where is she, your mother? Whatever has she been doing with herself all these years?"

There was a hush in the room, with whispered conversation swirling around us, and all eyes were turned toward me. The talk was about Lily and me and the tall young man.

"Thank you, ma'am," I said, ignoring her question. "Mr. Bottle designed my dress," I said, introducing him.

"Is he your brother?" she asked quizzically, looking as if she were adding numbers together in her head.

"He's a Bottle; I'm a Basket," I said in merriment at her bewildered look.

"Horace, please," he said, clicking his heels and tilting his head in a polite bow.

She turned her attention to him. "It makes her look quite different, a different child. . . . It's like seeing a ghost. . . ."

"She's very real, I assure you, madame," Horace said.

"About her mother . . . it's most unkind of Lily not to be in touch with us, her dearest childhood friends. . . ."

"Lovely table, madame," Horace said, breaking in. "Elegant. If I may . . ."

"Thank heaven for the food, yes, but the rain has ruined much of the fun," Mrs. Vandermeer said. "We've other things to play indoors—conundrums for the children and, thankfully, the palm readings for everyone and—"

"Mother," Ivy said, coming over, giving me a rather worried look. "She was supposed to come alone."

"Oh, Ivy," Mrs. Vandermeer said with a forced laugh. "A guest is allowed an escort."

"But Mother, you didn't tell me," Ivy said angrily.

Horace wagged his head. "Ivy, you must respect your elders," he said, shaking a finger at her. Gallantly, he took Mrs. Vandermeer's arm and steered her away toward the table. "Do show me the table, dear heart," he said serenely.

"She doesn't look like an Indian or a boy, Ivy Victoria," one of the girls said, looking me over. She had lovely black hair done in soft ringlets.

"But I am quite savage," I said, forgetting that only a moment before I had wished to be kind and good like Ma. "Honestly."

"Told you so, Sally," Ivy said. "She won't tell you anything either; she'll only make threats." Ivy grabbed the girl's arm and, as she dragged her away, looked back with an anxious look. I smiled and tugged on a lock of my hair, which made Ivy gasp.

Horace was now surrounded by a sea of plump matronly arms, and I caught a few snippets about fashion and food. Horace was a success, and I was on my own. Nearly everyone was staring at me or at Horace, though trying to hide it with their fans. So much for etiquette; it was hogwash, like Jasper had said.

Sally, the girl with black ringlets, came back. "You shouldn't have said that about the scalping to Ivy Victoria, you know. She's terrified of you now. Thinks you might *off* her." Sally smiled. "Does it run in the family . . . offing people?"

For a minute I couldn't breathe.

"Well, does it?" she asked.

I stared right at her, stared like Grandmother had taught me never to do. "Yes, it does," I said slowly, without blinking. "But only for sport, not for gain like everyone thinks. That *is* what all of you think, isn't it?"

Sally wet her lips and nodded. "So, something did happen. Right over there," she said, looking toward Grandmother's house, but I couldn't tell if she was playing along or believing it.

"Buried in the vegetable garden, to be exact." Several of the guests nearby leaned in to eavesdrop. In a loud whisper I said, "The bones make the vegetables delightfully crunchy." People caught their breath and moved away from us. I smiled.

Sally tilted her head, considering me carefully. "You've no doubt just ruined all your chances of ever being part of this set or of being invited anywhere important."

"But I am invited," I pointed out. "I wouldn't have come otherwise."

"You don't know much, do you?" she said, smiling a little too happily.

I was beginning to see why Ma, so kind and gentle, had wanted to run away from this sort of place and why going out among people was so fearful to her. Running away would not be hard to do right now.

But Sally stuck next to me and even moved the seating arrangements at the table so that we were together at the opposite end from Ivy.

"My mother said that your mother, Lily, was a rare beauty in heart and face but much too shy to ever be a success in society," she said when we were seated. "She said to ask you about your father. . . . Who is he, what is he, exactly?"

"You can tell your mother and all of them that I'm not like Lily," I said evenly. "Not kind, not sweet, not good. I'm like him, my father, fierce like a hawk." Stronger than a hawk flying in a gale wind, I thought, remembering Pa's parting words.

I looked for Horace, hoping he would come to my rescue, but the mothers and Horace were seated in chairs that lined the walls of the room. They were questioning him about my mother, too, no doubt. I was sure Horace would charm them without giving away one thing. Dear old Horace.

"So, tell me, what happened to your mother?" Sally said, lowering her voice to a whisper just after we were served our cake. "Why did she vanish? I promise not to tell the rest of them. You and I might be friends, you know."

I didn't believe that she meant to be friends at all. She was just another sort like Ivy, only smarter.

I took a small bite and licked my lips in a yummy sort of way to tease, before saying anything to Sally. "You first," I said. "Tell me all about everyone here. I want to know every little bit of mean gossip about everyone. Our secret, of course. Then I'll tell you whatever you want to know."

Sally lowered her lashes. "I'll tell you something," she whispered.

And my heart pounded fiercely, thrilled because she meant to tell me a secret, something quite dark.

Sally glanced around her, then motioned for me to lean closer. "They said your mother watched it happen," she whispered in my ear. "You know—what they did to your grandfather. They said that maybe she helped."

I could feel the blood drain from my face. "They said that?" No wonder Ma had said that Kingston was too far away to go back to, forever and ever. No wonder she was so mistrustful of others. I choked on a sob. Oh, Ma, how could they say that to you?

"You might learn the truth from Madame Blatzinsky about . . . you know, what really happened to your grandfather," Sally said. "She might see it in your palm. She really can tell things, true things about your life. Are you afraid?"

"No," I said, though I was, terribly. I knew Ma had not murdered anyone. But now I didn't feel sure about anyone else.

"As soon as the games begin, we'll go. I'll even go first," she said.

"All right," I said. Still, the black feeling I got in my stomach was starting to surge up in warning, when Sally led me down a long corridor away from Horace to Madame Blatzinsky.

# CHAPTER EIGHTEEN

Walking into the room at the end of the corridor with Sally was like walking into dusk. Pale light flickered through globes of frosted blue, frightful shadows wavered on the ceiling and darkly paneled walls, and heavy indigo velvet draped the windows. A few girls and their mothers, including Ivy and her mother, sat with Madame Blatzinsky at a round table in the center of the room.

The door clicked shut behind me. There was a rustling of gowns and the hush of whispery voices. Feverish, expectant eyes turned to look at me, waiting, as if they had been sitting and waiting for years for my arrival. I glanced at Ivy, questioningly, but all she did was smirk. With a very sick feeling, I knew I was captured, and the frightful, unspeakable things that Madame had seen in my hand were about to be revealed to all.

Madame Blatzinsky straightened. "We can begin," she said. It was the first time I had seen her without her veils. She was very old, with loose, saggy skin ringing her dark, protruding eyes. "Come closer, dear. Take the place by my side," she said in a soothing voice, beckoning with a fleshy finger. I took the empty chair next to her, and Sally sat on the other side of me.

"Place your hands on the table and join them together to form a circle," she said. "The circle must not be broken." Once again, I felt the strength in her fingers as she grasped my hand. But the idea of a circle was not a scary thing, and I took heart. Reading palms must surely be different when there were lots of people. But then everything changed.

Madame grew very still and slumped in her chair. "Are there any spirits present?" she asked. "Welcome."

A chill went down my spine; the skin prickled at the

back of my neck. This wasn't a harmless palm reading; this was a séance, and I was pretty sure I knew why.

Everyone sat still. It was so quiet that my breathing seemed loud, and I tried to be less noisy about it. I glanced quickly around the table. Everyone was looking at Madame B. Her head was tilted back and her eyes were quite rolled up in her head like she was in a faint or a seizure of some sort.

The room turned cold, very cold, so that our breath became vaporous. The lights flickered and burned low, and a stream of cool wind played across my hands.

"I'm sensing a spirit now, a spirit coming near, the spirit of a murdered man."

No one spoke. "The man is older. A grandfather, perhaps. I see something to do with the river. Paper money is falling through his fingers into the water. Does this mean anything to anyone here?"

My heart thudded dully. Surely they could hear it. I—we all, probably—knew that the spirit was meant to be my grandfather, losing Grandmother's fortune. It was a cruel hoax, a horrid joke to make a fool of me.

In a hushed voice, Sally spoke to the air. "She wants to know how you died, sir."

"Speak to us," Madame said. Then, in a quavery voice, she asked, "What do you want with me?"

"Ask him how he was murdered, Hattie," Ivy whispered.

I looked around the table at the barely disguised looks of delicious glee. I seethed like a roiling river. I started to get up, to laugh in their faces at the feeble hoax, but the wind that had been playful suddenly raged like a whirlwind. The indigo draperies billowed, a glass globe smashed to the floor, and the table began to rise, then thumped down hard. The others at the table hissed loudly. Sally clenched my hand tightly.

"Spirit, do you have a message for someone in the room?" Madame asked.

The room grew calm. I caught the sweet scent of a ripe plum, the sound of small thrumming wings. A ball of light, like an iridescent bubble, appeared above the center of the table and floated toward me. The orb of light circled around and around me, humming, giving off a glow of enormous love that warmed me. A love I knew. This was no hoax. The people in the room seemed to fade away.

"I have looked for you everywhere, little mouse, and here you are," came a ghostly whisper. "I am in the light, where it is beautiful, and I am well again. Nothing hurts me now."

Warmth coursed through my chilled arms and legs and went straight to the center of my heart. *Oh, Ma, why did you die?* I sobbed inside.

"So sorry, my child, sorry that I wasn't strong enough to live in the visible world. But Father is not here. They should know that your grandmother wouldn't hurt anyone, not my angel in the world, nor Rose. Ask and ye shall receive. Asssk," the voice said as it faded and the light grew smaller and smaller until it was gone. The gaslights flared up again, Madame Blatzinsky loosened her grip, and the circle was broken. Sally drew away from me.

"Was that really Hattie's mother?" Ivy asked, sounding afraid.

"Why didn't you inform me about the ball of light and that voice?" Mrs. Vandermeer said angrily to Madame Blatzinsky. "You've frightened all of us with your charlatan tricks. I thought we agreed—" She broke off, her nostrils flaring. "The price of the broken globe will come out of your purse."

Madame shrugged and looked unperturbed. She flashed me a wise look. "We have witnessed a beautiful thing today," she said. "Can't any of you accept that it was a miracle?"

Mrs. Vandermeer just glared. "Come, everyone. Let's proceed to the ballroom."

Without a word, the others fled the room ahead of their hostess, rustling off in their fat pink gowns like well-fed rats, back to the gay light of the party. Then it was just we three.

Sally was the first to speak. "Your mother is dead?"

I nodded.

"You might have told us," Sally said, looking hurt.

"It's easier not to tell," I said. "Besides, do you think it would have made a difference to this lot?"

Sally studied me. "Not all of us are like Ivy and her mother, you know."

"But how could I know that?"

"You couldn't," Sally agreed. She bit her lip and glanced toward the door before continuing. "I'm sorry for what they tried to do to you." Then she got up and left the room. When she had disappeared, I turned to Madame Blatzinsky. "Thank you," I said. "I'm very glad to know that my mother is well now."

"It's rare to truly make contact with the other world,"

Madame said. "I was touched that her gentle spirit would come to you."

"Yet you pretended my grandfather's spirit was here? Why? Why would you agree to such a terrible hoax?"

"I was wrong. I'm sorry." She shrugged. "I give them what they want; they keep my purse well lined. But today, a miracle. It is no small thing, child."

"It was a miracle," I said, still feeling the warm glow of my mother's love.

Madame winked. "I suspect you have many angels, child. So, little wild bird, you've been set free. Your mother has had the last word and can rest peacefully, free of the past," she said. "It's over."

"For them it is," I said, my anger burning again. "But not for me, not yet." I got up and walked straight through the glittering ballroom, a sea of gowns making way and giving me wide berth. Everyone watched me with the silent cold fury born of losing. No one tried to stop me from leaving, not even Horace.

# CHAPTER NINETEEN

Fire blazed in my chest now as I hurried back to Grandmother's from the séance. Proper etiquette was burnt to ashes by the time I stormed into the library, where Rose and Grandmother were having tea. "Where is Grandfather?" I demanded.

"Why do you ask?" Grandmother said, cautiously calm.

"What have you done with him? If he isn't buried in the garden or bricked up in the cellar, if you didn't murder him, what became of him? Where is he? Why is he such an unspeakable secret?"

Grandmother and Rose leapt to their feet in alarm. "Murdered?" Rose blustered. "Who said that?"

"Me . . . I did. And everyone else. They even said it to my mother, accused her of helping. Is that what you call etiquette? Is this the protocol of genteel society?"

I guess I hit them with too many things at once, because they both looked stunned and simply sat down again, and I rushed on.

"I found bones in the radish roots along with the keys."

"Oh, dear," Grandmother said, worrying the lace at her collar into a rumpled mess.

Rose looked quite stricken. "You thought we were murderers?"

"I certainly thought *you* were. Why wouldn't I?" I said hotly. "Always accusing me of being a sneak, of being a mongrel."

"Oh, dear, what have they done to you?" Grandmother said. "What happened over there?"

"It doesn't matter. What matters is what they did to my mother. What matters is that no one around here seems to know how to be kind or to tell the truth. About Grandfather or about anything."

It was quiet except for the ticking of the clocks.

"I have some money saved from my rafting trip," I said firmly. "I think it's enough to pay my passage home."

Grandmother's eyes filled, and tears slipped down her face. Rose's eyes snapped, became dark and broody. She flapped her arms, crossing them over her chest like folded-up wings, and drew away.

"I've spoiled everything again," Grandmother said. "I only wanted you to be happy here and make friends, not have any worries. I didn't ever suppose they would make you suffer for the past."

"But they did, Grandmother. You must have known they would."

Grandmother was silent. She started to crumple. "I did hope things would be different now."

"Grandmother," I said, going to sit by her. "I know you wanted things to go well for me. But I don't belong here."

She patted my hand. "Hattie, dear," she said finally, "I think it likely . . . I do believe the bones you found with the keys may be a bit of your grandfather."

And when she said that so cold and queerly, a chill went through me and raised the hair on the back of my head. I drew in a shaky breath and let it out slowly. "Did you . . . murder him?" I asked, giving both of them a long, dark look.

"I think it best if I start from the beginning," Grandmother said. But before she could go on, we heard the front door open and Rose rushed out, probably to waylay Horace and redirect him to the kitchen and, no doubt, to find out what he knew. I was glad it was just Grandmother and me now.

"Your grandfather was a gentle, thoughtful man," Grandmother said. "He loved to play with his little girl, our Lily. He enchanted her with stories of little folk and fairies. He could throw his voice and change it to seem like invisible folk were speaking from corners, or from behind cabinets or draperies. It was joyous fun and, in her younger years, quite harmless. Oh, what whimsy he dreamt up for Lily," Grandmother said with real affection. "Truly he delighted all of us and made us laugh. I can't actually say when his whimsical make-believe began to change and become real for him. Maybe, to some degree, it always had been.

"It's true that he made poor business investments and, without intervention in the business by my cousin, we would have lost everything. It did something to William.

He was different . . . angry and brooding. He became delusional and imagined horrible things instead of gentle fairy folk. He accused us of trying to poison him to get rid of the 'millstone,' and he did chop off a finger and hide it 'where it wouldn't hurt him anymore.' He talked nonsense, but even in his nonsense, he seemed desperate to tell me something. But the others, the voices in his head, may have drowned out all that was left of his real self.

"We managed through all of that, kept it secret, but one day, he turned violent. He slashed the paintings, the dear family portraits, even his own, even Lily's—shouting at them to stop staring and whispering and saying bad things about him."

"So where is he now? Did he die?"

"He's not dead, Hattie. Cousin Ernest and I moved him to a place where he could be properly looked after."

"You put him away somewhere?" I said as the shock of it bolted through me. "He's alive? In an asylum?"

"All of society have dark, unmentionable secrets," Grandmother said. "I thought keeping the secret about William's illness and his whereabouts would protect your mother and allow her to maintain her rightful place in society. But I was wrong."

I pushed on. "Instead . . . they taunted my mother.

They accused her of taking part in a murder." I stopped and tried to make a picture of it in my head. It wasn't hard.

Grandmother nodded. "None of the gossip about Grandfather being 'offed,' as you say, had yet reached us. At my persuasion, she accepted an invitation to a gala event being held in the ballroom of one of our hotels. She was too frightened and confused to stand up to them. Your father saved her, blazed out in fury against them when they tormented her with accusations and suspicion. He was all tenderness to her, your father— genuine, innocent, strong."

When she said that about Pa, my heart leapt up, and I longed to be safe with him again. "And he danced with her," I said. "Ma told me that he did and they fell in love."

Grandmother put her arms around me. "Hattie, dear," she said. "I was a foolish woman, so sure of my place in society and of my own importance, more sure of my daughter's love than anything in the world. If only I had known about the gossip, I might have protected her. . . . All I ever wanted was to keep her safe. But even the truth wouldn't have helped. They would still have broken her. I lost her and she never came back. And here we are, quiet broken pieces of lives once whole."

"She wanted to come back, Grandmother. She longed to come back to *you,* but she couldn't even leave our cabin and woods," I said. "Did you blame Pa for that, her not coming back? Was that why you were so . . . so frosty to him?"

Grandmother bowed her head. "I blamed your father for a great many things, for being the wrong sort for my daughter. Perhaps I blamed him for everything. But mostly, I resented him for saving my girl when I couldn't. But that day when he came here with you, that was different. After all those years, not knowing anything . . . and there you were so strong and bright and fierce and whole, and I forgave him everything. I wanted him gone, yes—gone before he could change his mind and take you away."

I hugged Grandmother and forgave her everything, too. But my heart had flown home to Pa.

# CHAPTER TWENTY

For weeks after the party, there was no consoling Horace. He was convinced that he had been such a great success that the invitations would come pouring in. He checked the letterbox several times a day for an invite, but day after day nothing was dropped through, not a trickle of anything. We were clearly left to ourselves, just as Sally had warned.

"I don't understand," he said.

"You truly were a success," I reassured him.

"Well . . . yes, I was," he said, "which makes it even more difficult to understand."

"Well, we gave it a try," he said after three weeks had passed and nothing came.

"You'll get over it, Horace," I said, keeping private my own worries about why I hadn't heard from Pa. I'd written weeks ago, but no letters had come. "You're a wonderful tutor, Horace," I continued. "Look how well I've done."

"Yes, I am quite good, aren't I? But you are a clever girl. Anyone might have taught you," he muttered. "And we haven't attempted chemistry yet, so you don't know."

It was unlike Horace to ever admit to not being good at something, so I ignored this as pure melancholy and went on. "And you're a poet. When would you write if you were always out at teas and parties or planning and readying for them? You'd never get a word written and you've gotten quite as good as Kingston's own Mr. Abbey," I said.

The tutor brightened for a moment. "Do you think so, really? You're not just being kind for my sake?"

I shook my head. "You must stick to it, Horace."

"That's what Madame Blatzinsky told me. She said I'd never accomplish a thing if I didn't settle my mind on something. But the cakes," he said mournfully. "The lovely cakes and all those confections. And it's gone so dead quiet over there. No one seems to be about except for the gardener and the master. Even Madame Blatzinsky hasn't been by in a fortnight. It's all so queer."

Madame Blatzinsky and confections were the least of my worries, and I was glad to put Ivy and the lot of them right out of my mind. But why didn't Pa write? And nothing had come from Jasper either. I hoped that I was not forgotten or that Pa had not taken sick. I had written twice more, just short, cheery notes with only a little line of begging and homesickness stuck in. How had Grandmother stood it all those years, never hearing a word, not even knowing about me till I was nearly grown?

Before Pa had left, he said he might get here for a visit before winter settled in, but now the geese were honking overhead and the leaves were falling in drifts, and the days were short and the mornings crisp. And still no word from Pa. November was not far off, and flurries of snow had whitened the ground on more than one occasion. It seemed as if winter was determined to come early.

And then, unannounced, Cousin Ernest showed up, wearing a very long face. He said only one word about business in my presence, "Cornell." After he left, Grandmother sat for a long while white-faced and shaking. She looked very old to me, withered like a dried-up leaf. But she didn't speak of the visit until after teatime, when we were all in the library.

"You've all probably guessed by now that the business has not recovered from our summer losses. My father's shipping line has dwindled to near nothing. We've had major repairs and fewer patrons."

"What shall we do, Grandmother?" I asked. As usual, I was thinking about myself. What if she had to send me home? But how could I go? I'd no word from Pa.

Grandmother studied the walls. "I've sold everything that's worth anything. We've made do with little, increased our self-sufficiency by growing more of our own food, doing our own gardening, doing without maids and gardeners, even turned the Vandermeer child's gowns into napkins and pillow covers. But now . . ."

"You're going to dismiss me, aren't you?" Horace said, looking up. As usual, his fingers were inky from writing his evening sonnets. "I don't want to leave. I've no family, and I don't care to go back to the city. It doesn't agree with me."

"I'm not dismissing you, Horace. We've all grown so fond of you, but I just can't afford to pay you any longer, and I'm afraid that our Hattie will not go to Academy; I can't pay the tuition. You've both worked wonderfully hard, but I'm afraid it's common school, after all."

I laid my studies aside and went over to sit next to her on the chaise. "I don't mind about common school," I said. "But can't we keep Horace?"

"I wouldn't put him out, if that's what you mean."

Horace looked woeful, but then he brightened. "I'm a clever teacher. Perhaps I could secure a position at one of the schools; there are so many. I could stay on then and pay you board."

Grandmother looked horrified at the mention of taking in a boarder. "I don't know. It wouldn't be proper."

"Who's proper?" Rose said with a chortle. "We gave up proper when she came. We're completely done with social customs, and about time, too. Besides, Horace is like family to me."

"To all of us," I said, and Grandmother nodded.

Horace glowed, actually, and looked around at all of us with great fondness, and I completely forgot why I'd ever thought Rose hardhearted.

"Well," Grandmother said, her color getting rosy now, "that settles quite a few things." She caught her breath and let it out slowly. "It's time now for my monthly visit to William. I mustn't delay or winter may suddenly descend and the trip become impossible."

Winter was a sad reminder that Pa hadn't written and likely wouldn't be coming for a visit. "We wouldn't want Grandfather to think he was forgotten," I said, thinking more of my feelings, really, than those of the grandfather I didn't know or have any particular fondness for.

"No, it wouldn't do," Grandmother said.

"Might I go with you?" I asked.

"You wouldn't be afraid?"

I thought of all the things I'd been through—Ma dying, the trip down the Delaware on the log raft over falls and rapids, seeing a boy drown, and then being left here, the rumors of murder, Ivy's party . . . "No," I said, "I won't be afraid."

# CHAPTER TWENTY-ONE

It was November when Grandmother and I finally went to visit Grandfather. We set out before daybreak with a lunch basket, books for the train, and Rose's teacakes as a special treat for him.

Horace was to spend the day going out to apply for a position at the papers. He'd not had any luck so far at the schools, because everything was filled for the semester.

At least the weather was agreeable—stars were still shining, and the sky was turning a soft shade of peach, which soon turned to a fiery orange crackling in the leafless trees. We took the train north to Albany and west to Utica, then took a coach to the asylum. Grandmother and I said little on the trip. We read, and I taught her how to do a social study of the passengers. But there was no one of much interest this cold November morning, no one but a pretentious, jabot-necked pheasant with a monocle to report about to Horace.

By the time we arrived at the gates of the asylum, the sun was warm and already moving toward the west. The building was massive, serious looking, with great thick pillars, barred windows like a prison, and a high wooden fence surrounding it. Several people were out walking on the grounds, and I wondered if they were lunatics.

Pouring out through the doors, as we came up, was a noisy group of schoolboys laughing about the looneys. "I am the Messiah come to save you," one boy called gleefully. He spread his arms wide. "Repent, you sinners!" The boys roared as they ran out to their waiting coaches.

Grandmother grasped my free hand. "It's horrible how they allow good people to be made such spectacles of ridicule," she said in a voice that sparked. "I have written countless letters, but they still persist in this barbaric, demeaning practice, allowing the patients here to be mocked by anyone—schoolboys, vacationers, curious passersby." She slipped an arm around my shoulder.

"Some of them think they are God?" I asked in surprise.

Grandmother nodded. "You may see and hear strange things, but you'll be fine, Hattie Belle," she said with a fond look. "I wouldn't have brought you if you weren't strong. There's nothing of the timid little mouse in you, my little mouse."

"No," I agreed, glad that Grandmother knew that about me. I was not afraid. I was curious, though, and tingled right to my fingertips.

Mr. Gray, the administrator, greeted Grandmother with warm congeniality. "He's having a good day, Mrs. Greymoor, quite docile. Not sedated much," he added in a warning sort of tone.

"I'll keep that in mind, Mr. Gray," Grandmother said.

He nodded. "I'll have an attendant show you up to the second ward."

The first floor was pleasant, with men sitting quietly or reading, playing cards or taken up in conversation. Paintings covered the walls and colorful rugs the floors. No one claimed to be God. It did not seem like such a bad place, but Grandmother told me it was the only ward where tourists were allowed.

Grandfather was in the next ward up, because Grandmother didn't want him exposed to the curious eyes of the public and because the first ward was more than she could afford. When we stepped into the open hall of the second ward, Grandmother pointed him out to me.

He was sitting quietly in a spot of sun, and when we came quite near, he caught sight of Grandmother, but his face did not change. I caught my breath and swallowed hard. I hadn't expected to see the faded sweetness in an older, lined face that was so much like Ma's. I swallowed again to keep back a sob. How awful if Ma had come to this. Maybe she had seen it coming, had worried that she would turn into him. Maybe that's why she quit on us, quit taking the cure for her pleurisy. She quit, thinking she would save us from her madness. Was that why we couldn't console her when she had felt the spiders crawling on her? Was it then that she knew for sure that she was slipping into madness, something not magical like her pretends? Did she fear that she would become violent like Grandfather had? My poor good sweet mother who, even in her growing madness, despaired of ever hurting those she loved.

"Horses," he said, and still there was no change in his face. His eyes looked empty, as if he were a doll, and he sat still and strangely frozen. He moved an arm up to his face stiffly, like a marionette being pulled by strings.

"Yes, William," she said. "I've brought someone special to meet you. This is Hattie Belle. She's our very own granddaughter."

"The thing is, we're not told. Doesn't matter. Rose water in the oatmeal," he said, looking empty. "Something should change. I've tried to do everything *they* say, but *they* won't stop. *They're* taking my organs for research now. Special. Very secret to change the world and bring back the sun."

"William?" she said gently. "This is Lily's child. William, this is our Hattie."

Grandfather put his arm down in the same puppetlike way. "I've lost mine. It was stolen."

"Grandfather," I said, copying Grandmother's soft tone. My heart raced at the queer way he spoke and the dead look on his face. "I'm your Hattie." And I noticed his other hand then, the one with the missing little finger.

"They're whispering and coming out of the walls. Blue eyes," he said, but his face rigid, his eyes blank. "If I had my hat, they wouldn't say those lies about me."

Grandfather saw me, but he didn't seem to know if I was real or not, or even what I was. Had he ever been this way with Ma? Yes, of course he had been. Grandmother had said so. And finally, the last piece of the puzzle about Ma and her fears fell into place. But I was not afraid of Grandfather's strangeness. Not in any way. I was strong like Pa, like a hawk in a storm that didn't falter even when blown off course.

"Look here, William," Grandmother said gently. "Rose has made your favorite cakes."

"Cakes?" Grandfather said. "Horse cakes. Poison. At least the bed is soft all the time."

I blinked and looked away. Seeing my sweet mother in Grandfather's lunacy was the saddest thing of all.

Grandmother took my arm. "I'll bring you something nice next time, William."

"Hats are safe. The blue hat will do," he said, and I hoped that he meant me.

I was glad when we started our journey home, glad when Grandmother slipped her arm around me again and I could lay my head against her dear, broken heart.

# CHAPTER TWENTY-TWO

Several days after we returned from visiting Grandfather, I wrote a short letter to Pa and posted it the same day:

November 7, 1883

Dear Pa,

Grandmother has told me everything I wanted to know. Grandfather did not die; he was away in a rest home for people with troubled minds. After seeing Grandfather, I think I understand a lot more about Ma. I don't think she could help quitting on us, Pa. Whatever made her give up was something darker and deeper than we knew, something we can't rightly know. I'm glad I have Ma's fine voice, but it doesn't matter that I'm not lovely and sweet like she was. I'd rather be strong like you, Pa, strong enough to fly home again.

My hair is below my shoulders again and Grandmother has taught me to put a little curl in the ends and I pull some of the straying locks back and tie a purple ribbon in it for Ma, who will always be our angel.

I have done very well with my studies and I will be going to common school again in January. The tutor is staying on with us. He has gotten a teaching position at one of the schools here, since one of the teachers got married and will not be returning after the Christmas recess.

I am growing up fast. I fear that if you don't come visit soon, you might not know me, because I am getting girlish looking enough to please even me. I know you have so much work to do before winter, Pa, but I sure could use a letter from home. I'm worried that something bad has happened to you. Please have Jasper write even a line or two and let me know how you are faring; then I won't worry anymore if I don't hear from you till spring.

Grandmother said to let you know that you are always welcome to stay here whenever you can make it up for a visit. She doesn't hate you or blame you for anything . . . not anymore. I sure would be happy to see you. There is so much to tell you that should only be said face to face. I miss you, Pa.

Love from your girl,
*Hattie Belle*

I longed for the dark of the evergreen forest and the scent of fir and moss and dying ferns, and the whistle of the hawk gliding over the treetops, and I longed for even a word from Pa. But none came. Then winter settled in with a sharp, cold spell and a deep snow right after Thanksgiving. Ice floes formed on the Hudson, and sadly I knew Pa would not be coming.

# CHAPTER TWENTY-THREE

Before Christmas, the cold spell with snow and the low, overcast clouds drifted away. The sun came out, the snow melted, and the air held the freshness of spring. The lawn was turning yellowish, but a few violets sprinkled the gardens with color, and the leaves of the vinca vines were a stronger, deeper shade of green.

At midday, when the sun was the warmest, I walked out on the paths around the gardens, then out on the soggy lawn to the far western edge of the property. I hung on the picket fence and looked with sick longing toward the hills and scanned the sky for a circling hawk, but there was no sign. I stood with tears popping out of my eyes.

Then I heard it, the long, shrill whistle of a hawk. I glanced quickly up at the sky, but there was nothing. I rushed back to the walk and scanned the avenue in all directions, but still there was nothing. With a hope close to fear, I whistled long and shrill and high.

The whistle came back in answer and I saw him, my pa, wearing his good suit, striding up the bluestone walk. "Pa," I called. "Pa!" I waved my arms and ran toward him. "Oh, Pa, you've come at last!"

When I reached him, he grabbed me up in his arms. "My girl," he said with a catch in his voice. "My own Hattie Belle."

I buried my face against the rough wool of his suit and squeezed him hard for a long time.

When we went inside, Grandmother was warm and gracious to Pa, Rose was a complete buzzard, Horace stared in awe as if Pa had sprung from the pages of a Whitman poem, and Pa was restless before he had even settled into a chair.

Pa had barely been poured his tea, when he scuffled

his feet under the table and pain lined his face. "Hortensia," he said. "I'd like to be alone with Hattie."

I had wanted to be alone with Pa myself, although I hadn't known how to say it politely. Now it was done for me. The dark, hooded scowls from Rose were very buzzardy and clearly said that she did not understand, did not like Pa being here. She leaned toward me as I lifted my cup and saucer and stood. "Always knew you were a breaker," she whispered.

"Of course, Amos," Grandmother said, though I saw her eyes and mouth crinkle up in worry. "I quite understand."

In the library, Pa sat across from me, his back to the clocks. He was never one for small talk, and he came straight to the point now. "Hattie Belle, I've come to take you home."

Rose's words came back suddenly, like a hard slap—breaker of valuable things. I was about to break something valuable, a great many things maybe. I sat across from Pa on Grandmother's chaise and bowed my head.

"Thought you'd want to come home," Pa said, and I could hear the pain in his voice like an echo from my heart. "I built you a room on the cabin, put in a real wood floor and some windows. Got a letter for you right here in my pocket from a good friend, too," Pa said, fetching it out and handing it over to me.

Inside the envelope was a store-bought card. The card had a picture of a Christmas tree, decorated with glowing candles and all sorts of angels. Presents were under the tree. Children and parents were off to one side holding hands, smiling or singing. A window showed snow fluttering down and a darkened silhouette of Saint Nicholas shouldering a full bundle of toys. I ran my fingers over the beautiful scene and thought about the fine boy who had chosen it for me. Inside, Jasper had written a note:

Dear Hattie,

Isn't it the best news that you're coming home for Christmas? I would've come along with your Pa, but I guess he wanted some time with you by himself first. Can't blame him for that. You're coming at just the right time when there's a recess from school and we can catch up on things, and I know we've both got a lot of news to share though mine's probably not as exciting as yours.

We're planning a big celebration on account of you coming back and inviting you to come over and have Christmas dinner with us. You can help my sisters make cookies if you want, though mainly, I know you'd rather go skating and sledding with me. I'll be waiting for the stagecoach with you on it.

Your best friend,

*Jasper*

If there were ever words written that felt like joy, Jasper's good words were it. If there was a sound that a heart makes when it gets broken in two, that was the sound in my chest right then. It took more than a minute for me to get my voice to come out. "It's a real fine letter, Pa," I said. "You know Jasper's always going to be my best friend."

Pa laughed and rubbed his cheek. "Ayah. Guess I know that's true all right. And Edith, she's nearly as eager as her brother Jasper and . . . and Amelia."

"Amelia?" I asked.

"You remember the schoolmarm, Hattie Belle. She started giving me reading and writing lessons so I could write you letters. Wanted to surprise you."

"That's a real fine thing, Pa," I said, feeling proud.

"Ayah." Pa guffawed. "Amelia and I got hitched a while back. Harvest time. We meant to write and tell you . . ."

"She's a real nice lady, Pa," I said, but it felt just like a big hand was squeezing my heart.

"She is at that. We got us a real family again, Hattie Belle. We'll be adding another come spring, a boy, maybe. Amelia says you can keep right on going to school. Her folks live in Downsville. You can board with them and come home weekends some and holidays."

I looked up at Pa then, and I could see how proud he was of figuring everything out just right for us, for him.

"Guess I should've writ to give you some time to think on it," Pa said.

"I've been real homesick, Pa. You know I want to go home," I said, without looking up. "I want to go with you right now." My heart thudded painfully. "Things never seem to go right here, but it'd be wrong for me to go off, leave like Ma did. I know Ma couldn't help it, but I can't leave, not yet, not for a while." I stopped and looked up again at Pa's strong face. "Grandmother's sort of like a good wool sock with a hole in it, Pa. That sock still has a lot of wear in it, but that hole is bound to get bigger if it isn't mended proper. She deserves that chance."

"That's a real fine way of putting it, Hattie Belle," Pa said.

"I'll always be your girl, Pa, and I'll always be a Hill Hawk no matter what, and I'll come back. You know I will, but it wouldn't be right for me to leave just yet."

Pa sat thoughtful for a minute with Great-Grandfather's clocks ticking away behind him like strong, gentle heart-beats. "Guess you're right about that, little un."

"Oh, Pa," I said, choking on a sob. "Guess it was hard like this for Ma, being caught between the ones she loved best. But I won't be gone forever—you know I won't. I'm like you, Pa. My heart is fierce and my wings are strong enough to fly me home."

Pa cupped my chin with one of his big hands and tilted it up and brushed my tears away. "I know that, Hattie Belle. I never doubted my girl for a second."

"It's a powerful lot to ask of you, Pa, but in the spring, after rafting's done, might I come home and stay for the summer? Maybe for good?"

Pa lit up bright as a full moon on a crisp winter night. "Ayah," he said. And it was enough.

When Pa left, it was nearly like before—the first time back in April, when he'd come to leave me here, me whistling to Pa, then biting my lip till I could taste blood when his hawk whistle came back long and high and shrill. Pa would be fine, I knew. Everybody would. Now the only broken heart was the one that was split between here and there.

I looked up at my Grandmother's gingerbread house, with its peeling paint outside and its worn rugs and chipped plates and tarnished brass inside. I went up the steps, and I smiled at those dear ones watching anxiously from the window. This was home for now; they were my family. And one day, not far off, I'd be whistling again, my strong wings carrying me back to my first home.

**Don't miss *Hill Hawk Hattie*,
Clara Gillow Clark's first novel
about Hattie Belle Basket.**

★ "Tough, conflicted, wry, and introspective, Hattie is an
ideal character to connect readers to the history. With
beautiful rhythmic sentences, the simple first-person
narrative captures her rustic innocence, the thrilling
rafting adventure, and the heartfelt struggle of a tough
girl who feels useful to her father only in the role of
a boy." —*Booklist* (starred review)

"This historical fiction novel is simultaneously
informative and moving. Neither the drama nor the
emotion is overwrought, and Hattie emerges as a
refreshingly honest, vibrant, complex character. . . .
Clark's novel will appeal to a wide audience of both
male and female readers seeking adventure and
history." —*Voice of Youth Advocates*

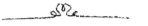

**Clara Gillow Clark** is the youngest child in a family who came from "a long line of farmers and readers," and—when she wasn't wanting to be an inventor, archaeologist, geologist, missionary, or solo violinist—grew increasingly drawn to writing. After marrying and having a son, she read a magazine article on children's author Judy Blume, who, like her, was a stay-at-home mom who sold her own crafts before starting her writing career. Inspired, Clara Gillow Clark began commuting to writing classes in New York City, while juggling jobs ranging from teacher's aide to store manager.

Her long efforts paid off. "Now I work at home," she says happily. When she's not writing—or reading, or teaching writing, or talking shop with other writers—she enjoys baking, gardening, and walking the dirt roads near her little red house, surrounded by her own meadows, woods, and lake.

Researching *Hill Hawk Hattie*, she says, was truly a labor of love. "The book takes place in the country of my heart, the Upper Delaware, where for many years I gathered materials to write a book about the old-time rafting era. Serendipitously, mysteriously, the story came flooding together one day when I was out walking on the dirt roads that border my property, and Hattie's voice rushed like a torrent into my head." Discovering the character of Hattie, the author says, "felt like a gift, this little girl with the powerful voice. Some days I had to pinch myself, I was so happy that she kept showing up to work with me."

About *Hattie on Her Way*, Clara Gillow Clark says, "Like Hattie, I attended a one-room school and lived in a rural area. Shortly after my father died, we moved to a town that seemed cold and frightening at first. In this new setting, I faced the challenge of being a tall misfit alongside petite girls who wore nice dresses and shiny shoes and knew the proper etiquette of birthday treats and valentines. Hattie's story is much tougher than my own, but we share many of the same emotional struggles, experiencing both loss and healing, and searching for sense and meaning in a topsy-turvy world.

"I hope kids take away some comfort and strength from Hattie's story," she continues, "including an understanding that sometimes the people closest to us have a hard time saying in words, 'I love you.' I want kids to know that everybody has tough times, but the only way to get through them is to go on."

Clara Gillow Clark lives and works in Lookout, Pennsylvania.